Michael,

> The story comes up different
> every time and has no ending
> but always begins with you.

ACKNOWLEDGMENTS

To my mother, Rita Gourneau Erdrich, friend and example, *chi migwitch*. I still hear your stories of reservation and bush life. I am indebted to Michael Dorris, who tracked moose near Tyonek, Alaska, and whose presence is of course inextricable from this story. Thanks also to my sister, Lise Erdrich Croonenberghs, for her sharp observations, and to Mary Lou Fox, of Manitoulin Island, Ontario. Along with the late Ben Gourneau, my great-uncle, a trapper and story-teller, I salute my grandfather, Patrick Gourneau, and the four branches of the Ojibwa Nation, those of strength, who endure.

CONTENTS

Winter 1912
Manitou-geezisohns
Little Spirit Sun

—

N A N A P U S H

We started dying before the snow, and like the snow, we continued to fall. It was surprising there were so many of us left to die. For those who survived the spotted sickness from the south, our long fight west to Nadouissioux land where we signed the treaty, and then a wind from the east, bringing exile in a storm of government papers, what descended from the north in 1912 seemed impossible.

By then, we thought disaster must surely have spent its force, that disease must have claimed all of the Anishinabe that the earth could hold and bury.

But the earth is limitless and so is luck and so were our people once. Granddaughter, you are the child of the invisible, the ones who disappeared when, along with the first bitter punishments of early winter, a new sickness swept down. The consumption, it was called by young Father Damien, who came in that year to replace the priest who succumbed to the same devastation as his flock. This disease was different from the pox and fever, for it came on slow. The outcome, however, was just as certain. Whole families of your relatives lay ill and helpless in its breath. On the reservation, where we were forced close together, the clans dwindled. Our tribe unraveled like a coarse rope, frayed at either end as the old and new among us were taken. My own family was wiped out one by one, leaving only Nanapush. And after, although I had lived no more than fifty winters, I was considered an old man. I'd seen enough to be one. In the years I'd passed, I saw more change than in a hundred upon a hundred before.

My girl, I saw the passing of times you will never know.

I guided the last buffalo hunt. I saw the last bear shot. I trapped the last beaver with a pelt of more than two years' growth. I spoke aloud the words of the government treaty, and refused to sign the settlement papers that would take away our woods and lake. I axed the last birch that was older than I, and I saved the last Pillager.

Fleur, the one you will not call mother.

We found her on a cold afternoon in late winter, out in your family's cabin near Matchimanito Lake, where my companion, Edgar Pukwan of the tribal police, was afraid to go. The water there was surrounded by the highest oaks, by woods inhabited by ghosts and roamed by Pillagers, who knew the secret ways to cure or kill, until their art deserted them. Dragging our sled into the clearing we saw two things: the smokeless tin chimney spout jutting from the roof, and the empty hole in the door where the string was drawn inside. Pukwan did not want to enter, fearing the unburied Pillager spirits might seize him by the throat and turn him windigo. So I was the one who broke the thin-scraped hide that made a window. I was the one who lowered himself into the stinking silence, onto the floor. I was also the one to find the old man and woman, your grandparents, the little brother and two sisters, stone cold and wrapped in gray horse blankets, their faces turned to the west.

Afraid as I was, stilled by their quiet forms, I touched each bundle in the gloom of the cabin, and wished each spirit a good journey on the three-day road, the old-time road, so well-trampled by our people this deadly season. Then something in the corner knocked. I flung the door wide. It was the eldest daughter, Fleur, about seventeen years old then. She was so feverish that she'd thrown off her covers, and now she huddled against the cold wood range, staring and shaking. She was wild as a filthy wolf, a big bony girl whose sudden bursts of strength and snarling cries terrified the listening Pukwan. So again I was the one who struggled to lash her to the sacks of supplies and to the boards of the sled. I wrapped more blankets over her and tied them down as well.

Pukwan kept us back, convinced he should carry out the Agency's instructions to the letter. He carefully nailed up the official quarantine sign, and then, without removing the bodies, he tried to burn down the house. But though he threw kerosene repeatedly against the logs and even started a blaze with birchbark and chips of wood, the flames narrowed and shrank, went out in puffs of smoke. Pukwan cursed and looked desperate, caught between his official duties and his fear of Pillagers. The last won out. He finally dropped the tinders and helped me drag Fleur along the trail.

And so we left five dead at Matchimanito, frozen behind their cabin door.

There are some who say Pukwan and I should have done right and buried the Pillagers first thing. They say the unrest and curse of trouble that struck our people in the years that followed was the doing of dissatisfied spirits. I know what's fact, and have never been afraid of talking. Our trouble came from living, from liquor and the dollar bill. We stumbled toward the government bait, never looking down, never noticing how the land was snatched from under us at every step.

When it came Edgar Pukwan's turn to draw the sled, he took off like devils chased him, bounced Fleur over potholes as if she were a log, and tipped her twice into the snow. I followed the sled, encouraged Fleur with songs, cried at Pukwan to watch for hidden branches and deceptive drops, and finally got her to my cabin, a small tightly tamped box overlooking the crossroad.

"Help me," I cried, cutting at the ropes, not even bothering with knots. Fleur closed her eyes, panted, and tossed her head side to side. Her chest rattled as she strained for air; she grabbed me around the neck. Still weak from my own sickness, I staggered, fell, lurched into my cabin wrestling the strong girl inside with me. I had no wind left over to curse Pukwan, who watched but refused to touch her, turned away, and vanished with the whole sled of supplies. It did not surprise or cause me enduring sorrow, later, when Pukwan's son, also named Edgar and also of the tribal police, told me that his father came home, crawled into bed, and took no food from that moment until his last breath passed.

As for Fleur, with each day she improved in small changes. First her gaze focused, and the next night her skin was cool and damp. She was clearheaded, and after a week she remembered what had befallen her family, how they had taken sick so suddenly, gone under. With her memory, mine came back, only too sharp. I was not prepared to think of the people I had lost, or to speak of them, although we did, carefully, without letting their names loose in the wind that would reach their ears.

We feared that they would hear us and never rest, come back out of pity for the loneliness we felt. They would sit in the snow outside the door, waiting until from longing we joined them. We would all be together on the journey then, our destination the village at the end of the road where people gamble day and night but never lose their money, eat but never fill their stomachs, drink but never leave their minds.

The snow receded long enough for us to dig the ground with picks.

As tribal police, Pukwan's son was forced by regulation to help bury the dead. So again we took the dark road to Matchimanito, the son leading rather than the father. We spent the day chipping at the earth until we had a hole long and deep enough to lay the Pillagers shoulder to shoulder. Then we covered them and built five small board houses. I scratched out their clan markers, four crosshatched bears and a marten, then Pukwan Junior shouldered the government's tools and took off down the path. I settled myself near the graves.

I asked those Pillagers, as I had asked my own children and wives, to leave us now and never come back. I offered tobacco, smoked a pipe of red willow for the old man. I told them not to pester their daughter just because she had survived, or to blame me for finding them, or Pukwan Junior for leaving too soon. I told them that I was sorry, but they must abandon us. I insisted. But the Pillagers were as stubborn as the Nanapush clan and would not leave my thoughts. I think they followed me home. All the way down the trail, just beyond the edges of my sight, they flickered, thin as needles, shadows piercing shadows.

The sun had set by the time I got back, but Fleur was awake, sitting in the dark as if she knew. She never moved to build up the fire, never asked where I had been. I never told her either, and as the days passed we spoke even less, always with roundabout caution. We felt the spirits of the dead so near that at length we just stopped talking.

This made it worse.

Their names grew within us, swelled to the brink of our lips, forced our eyes open in the middle of the night. We were filled with the water of the drowned, cold and black, airless water that lapped against the seal of our tongues or leaked slowly from the corners of our eyes. Within us, like ice shards, their names bobbed and shifted. Then the slivers of ice began to collect and cover us. We became so heavy, weighted down with the lead gray frost, that we could not move. Our hands lay on the table like cloudy blocks. The blood within us grew thick. We needed no food. And little warmth. Days passed, weeks, and we didn't leave the cabin for fear we'd crack our cold and fragile bodies. We had gone half windigo. I learned later that this was common, that there were many of our people who died in this manner, of the invisible sickness. There were those who could not swallow another bite of food because the names of their dead anchored their tongues. There were those who let their blood stop, who took the road west after all.

But one day the new priest, just a boy really, opened our door. A dazzling and painful light flooded through and surrounded Fleur and me. Another Pillager was found, the priest said, Fleur's cousin Moses was alive in the woods. Numb, stupid as bears in a winter den, we blinked at the priest's slight silhouette. Our lips were parched, stuck together. We could hardly utter a greeting, but we were saved by one thought: a guest must eat. Fleur gave Father Damien her chair and put wood on the gray coals. She found flour for gaulette. I went to fetch snow to boil for tea water, but to my amazement the ground was bare. I was so surprised that I bent over and touched the soft, wet earth.

My voice rasped at first when I tried to speak, but then, oiled by strong tea, lard and bread, I was off and talking. Even a sledge won't stop me once I start. Father Damien looked astonished, and then wary, as I began to creak and roll. I gathered speed. I talked both languages in streams that ran alongside each other, over every rock, around every obstacle. The sound of my own voice convinced me I was alive. I kept Father Damien listening all night, his green eyes round, his thin face straining to understand, his odd brown hair in curls and clipped knots. Occasionally, he took in air, as if to add observations of his own, but I pushed him under with my words.

I don't know when it was that your mother slipped out.

She was too young and had no stories or depth of life to rely upon. All she had was raw power, and the names of the dead that filled her. I can speak them now. They have no more interest in any of us. Old Pillager. Ogimaakwe, Boss Woman, his wife. Asasaweminikwesens, Chokecherry Girl. Bineshii, Small Bird, also known as Josette. And the last, the boy Ombaashi, He Is Lifted By Wind.

There was the other, a Pillager cousin named Moses. He had survived but, as they later said of Fleur, he didn't know where he was anymore, this place of reservation surveys or the other place, boundless, where the dead sit talking, see too much, and regard the living as fools.

And we were. Starvation makes fools of anyone. In the past, some had sold their allotment land for one hundred poundweight of flour. Others, who were desperate to hold on, now urged that we get together and buy back our land, or at least pay a tax and refuse the lumbering money that would sweep the marks of our boundaries off the map like a pattern of straws. Many were determined not to allow the hired surveyors, or even our own people, to enter the deepest bush. They spoke of the guides Hat and Many Women, now dead, who had taken the government pay.

But that spring outsiders went in as before, and some of us too. The purpose was to measure the lake. Only now they walked upon the fresh graves of Pillagers, crossed death roads to plot out the deepest water where the lake monster, Misshepeshu, hid himself and waited.

"Stay here with me," I said to Fleur when she came to visit.

She refused.

"The land will go," I told her. "The land will be sold and measured."

But she tossed back her hair and walked off, down the path, with nothing to eat till thaw but a bag of my onions and a sack of oats.

Who knows what happened? She returned to Matchimanito and stayed there alone in the cabin that even fire did not want. A young girl had never done such a thing before. I heard that in those months she was asked for fee money on all four allotments, even the island where Moses hid. The Agent went out there, then got lost, spent a whole night following the moving lights and lamps of people who would not answer him, but talked and laughed among themselves. They only let him go at dawn because he was so stupid. Yet he asked Fleur again for money, and the next thing we heard he was living in the woods and eating roots, gambling with ghosts.

Every year there are more who come looking for profit, who draw lines across the land with their strings and yellow flags. They disappear sometimes, and now there are so many betting with sticks and dice out near Matchimanito at night that you wonder how Fleur sleeps, or if she sleeps at all. Why should she? She does without so many things. The company of the living. Ammunition for her gun.

Some have ideas. You know how old chickens scratch and gabble. That's how the tales started, all the gossip, the wondering, all the things people said without knowing and then believed, since they heard it with their own ears, from their own lips, each word.

I was never one to take notice of the talk of those who fattened in the shade of the new Agent's storehouse. But I watched the wagons take the rutted turnoff to Matchimanito. Few of them returned, it is true, but those that did were enough, loaded high with hard green wood. From where we now sit, granddaughter, I heard the groan and crack, felt the ground tremble as each tree slammed earth. I weakened into an old man as one oak went down, another and another was lost, as a gap formed here, a clearing there, and plain daylight entered.

CHAPTER TWO

Summer 1913
Miskomini-geezis
Raspberry Sun

—

PAULINE

The first time she drowned in the cold and glassy waters of Matchimanito, Fleur Pillager was only a child. Two men saw the boat tip, saw her struggle in the waves. They rowed over to the place she went down, and jumped in. When they lifted her over the gunwales, she was cold to the touch and stiff, so they slapped her face, shook her by the heels, worked her arms and pounded her back until she coughed up lake water. She shivered all over like a dog, then took a breath. But it wasn't long afterward that those two men disappeared. The first wandered off and the other, Jean Hat, got himself run over by his own surveyor's cart.

It went to show, the people said. It figured to them all right. By saving Fleur Pillager, those two had lost themselves.

The next time she fell in the lake, Fleur Pillager was

fifteen years old and no one touched her. She washed on shore, her skin a dull dead gray, but when George Many Women bent to look closer, he saw her chest move. Then her eyes spun open, clear black agate, and she looked at him. "You take my place," she hissed. Everybody scattered and left her there, so no one knows how she dragged herself home. Soon after that we noticed Many Women changed, grew afraid, wouldn't leave his house and would not be forced to go near water or guide the mappers back into the bush. For his caution, he lived until the day that his sons brought him a new tin bathtub. Then the first time he used it he slipped, got knocked out, and breathed water while his wife stood in the other room frying breakfast.

Men stayed clear of Fleur Pillager after the second drowning. Even though she was good-looking, nobody dared to court her because it was clear that Misshepeshu, the water man, the monster, wanted her for himself. He's a devil, that one, love hungry with desire and maddened for the touch of young girls, the strong and daring especially, the ones like Fleur.

Our mothers warn us that we'll think he's handsome, for he appears with green eyes, copper skin, a mouth tender as a child's. But if you fall into his arms, he sprouts horns, fangs, claws, fins. His feet are joined as one and his skin, brass scales, rings to the touch. You're fascinated, cannot move. He casts a shell necklace at your feet, weeps gleaming chips that harden into mica on your breasts. He holds you under. Then he takes the body of a lion, a fat brown worm, or a familiar man. He's made of gold. He's made of beach moss. He's a thing of dry foam, a thing of death by drowning, the death a Chippewa cannot survive.

Unless you are Fleur Pillager. We all knew she couldn't

swim. After the first time, we thought she'd keep to herself, live quiet, stop killing men off by drowning in the lake. We thought she would keep the good ways. But then, after the second return, and after old Nanapush nursed her through the sickness, we knew that we were dealing with something much more serious. Alone out there, she went haywire, out of control. She messed with evil, laughed at the old women's advice and dressed like a man. She got herself into some half-forgotten medicine, studied ways we shouldn't talk about. Some say she kept the finger of a child in her pocket and a powder of unborn rabbits in a leather thong around her neck. She laid the heart of an owl on her tongue so she could see at night, and went out, hunting, not even in her own body. We know for sure because the next morning, in the snow or dust, we followed the tracks of her bare feet and saw where they changed, where the claws sprang out, the pad broadened and pressed into the dirt. By night we heard her chuffing cough, the bear cough. By day her silence and the wide grin she threw to bring down our guard made us frightened. Some thought that Fleur Pillager should be driven from the reservation, but not a single person who spoke like that had the nerve. And finally, when people were just about to get together and throw her out, she left on her own and didn't come back all summer. That's what I'm telling about.

During those months, when Fleur lived a few miles south in Argus, things happened. She almost destroyed that town.

When she got down to Argus in the year of 1913, it was just a grid of six streets on either side of the railroad depot. There were two elevators, one central, the other a few miles west. Two stores competed for the trade of the three hundred citizens, and three churches quarreled with one another for their souls. There was a frame building for Lutherans, a heavy brick one for Episcopalians, and a long narrow shingle Catholic church. This last had a slender steeple, twice as high as any building or tree.

No doubt, across the low flat wheat, watching from the road as she came near on foot, Fleur saw that steeple rise, a shadow thin as a needle. Maybe in that raw space it drew her the way a lone tree draws lightning. Maybe, in the end, the Catholics are to blame. For if she hadn't seen that sign of pride, that slim prayer, that marker, maybe she would have just kept walking.

But Fleur Pillager turned, and the first place she went once she came into town was to the back door of the priest's residence attached to the landmark church. She didn't go there for a handout, although she got that, but to ask for work. She got that too, or we got her. It's hard to tell which came out worse, her or the men or the town, although as always Fleur lived.

The men who worked at the butcher's had carved about a thousand carcasses between them, maybe half of that steers and the other half pigs, sheep, and game like deer, elk, and bear. That's not even mentioning the chickens, which were beyond counting. Pete Kozka owned the place, and employed three men: Lily Veddar, Tor Grunewald, and Dutch James.

I got to Argus through Dutch. He was making a mercantile delivery to the reservation when he met my father's sister Regina, a Puyat and then a Kashpaw through her first husband. Dutch didn't change her name right off, that came later. He never did adopt her son, Russell, whose father lived somewhere in Montana now.

13

During the time I stayed with them, I hardly saw Dutch or Regina look each other in the eye or talk. Perhaps it was because, except for me, the Puyats were known as a quiet family with little to say. We were mixed-bloods, skinners in the clan for which the name was lost. In the spring before the winter that took so many Chippewa, I bothered my father into sending me south, to the white town. I had decided to learn the lace-making trade from nuns.

"You'll fade out there," he said, reminding me that I was lighter than my sisters. "You won't be an Indian once you return."

"Then maybe I won't come back," I told him. I wanted to be like my mother, who showed her half-white. I wanted to be like my grandfather, pure Canadian. That was because even as a child I saw that to hang back was to perish. I saw through the eyes of the world outside of us. I would not speak our language. In English, I told my father we should build an outhouse with a door that swung open and shut.

"We don't have such a thing upon our house." He laughed. But he scorned me when I would not bead, when I refused to prick my fingers with quills, or hid rather than rub brains on the stiff skins of animals.

"I was made for better," I told him. "Send me down to your sister." So he did. But I did not learn to thread and work the bobbins and spools. I swept the floors in a butcher shop, and cared for my cousin Russell.

Every day I took him to the shop and we set to work—sprinkled fresh sawdust, ran a hambone across the street to a customer's beanpot or a package of sausage to the corner. Russell took the greater share of orders, worked the harder. Though young, he was fast, reliable. He never stopped to watch a cloud pass, or a spider secure a fly with the same quick care as Pete wrapped a thick steak for the doctor. Russell and I were different. He never sat to rest, never fell to wishing he owned a pair of shoes like those that passed on the feet of white girls, shoes of hard red leather decorated with cut holes. He never listened to what those girls said about him, or imagined them doubling back to catch him by the hand. In truth, I hardly rinsed through the white girls' thoughts.

That winter, we had no word from my family, although Regina asked. No one knew yet how many were lost, people kept no track. We heard that wood could not be sawed fast enough to build the houses for their graves, and there were so few people strong enough to work, anyway, that by the time they got around to it the brush had grown, obscuring the new-turned soil, the marks of burials. The priests tried to discourage the habit of burying the dead in trees, but the ones they dragged down had no names to them, just scraps of their belongings. Sometimes in my head I had a dream I could not shake. I saw my sisters and my mother swaying in the branches, buried too high to reach, wrapped in lace I never hooked.

I tried to stop myself from remembering what it was like to have companions, to have my mother and sisters around me, but when Fleur came to us that June, I remembered. I made excuses to work next to her, I questioned her, but Fleur refused to talk about the Puyats or about the winter. She shook her head, looked away. She touched my face once, as if by accident, or to quiet me, and said that perhaps my family had moved north to avoid the sickness, as some mixed-bloods did.

I was fifteen, alone, and so poor-looking I was invisible to most customers and to the men in the shop. Until they needed me, I blended into the stained brown walls, a skinny big-nosed girl with staring eyes.

From this, I took what advantage I could find. Because I could fade into a corner or squeeze beneath a shelf I knew everything: how much cash there was in the till, what the men joked about when no one was around, and what they did to Fleur.

Kozka's Meats served farmers for a fifty-mile radius, both to slaughter, for it had a stockpen and chute, and to cure the meat by smoking it or spicing it in sausage. The storage locker was a marvel, made of many thicknesses of brick, earth insulation, and Minnesota timber, lined inside with wood shavings and vast blocks of ice cut from the deepest end of Matchimanito, hauled down from the reservation each winter by horse and sled.

A ramshackle board building, part killing shed, part store, was fixed to the low square of the lockers. That's where Fleur worked. Kozka hired her for her strength. She could lift a haunch or carry a pole of sausages without stumbling, and she soon learned cutting from Fritzie, a string-thin blond who chain-smoked and handled the razor-edged knives with nerveless precision, slicing close to her stained fingers. The two women worked afternoons, wrapping their cuts in paper, and Fleur carried the packages to the lockers. Russell liked to help her. He vanished when I called, took none of my orders, but I soon learned that he could always be found alongside Fleur's hip, one hand gently pinching a fold of her skirt, so delicately that she could pretend not to notice.

Of course, she did. She knew the effect she had on men, even the very youngest of them. She swayed them, sotted them, made them curious about her habits, drew them close with careless ease and cast them off with the same indifference. She was good to Russell, it is true, even fussed about him like a mother, combed his hair with her fingers, and scolded me for kicking or teasing him.

Fleur poked bits of sugar between Russell's lips when we sat for meals, skimmed the cream from the jar when Fritzie's back was turned and spooned it into his mouth. For work, she gave him small packages to carry when she and Fritzie piled cut meat outside the locker's heavy doors, opened only at five P.M. each afternoon, before the men ate supper.

Sometimes Dutch, Tor, and Lily stayed at the lockers after closing, and when they did Russell and I stayed too, cleaned the floors, restoked the fires in the front smokehouse, while the men sat around the squat, cold cast-iron stove spearing slats of herring onto hardtack bread. They played long games of poker, or cribbage on a board made from the planed end of a salt crate. They talked. We ate our bread and the ends of sausages, watched and listened, although there wasn't much to hear since almost nothing ever happened in Argus. Tor was married, Dutch lived with Regina, and Lily read circulars. They mainly discussed the auctions to come, equipment, or women.

Every so often, Pete Kozka came out front to make a whist, leaving Fritzie to smoke her cigarettes and fry raised donuts in the back room. He sat and played a few rounds but kept his thoughts to himself. Fritzie did not tolerate him talking behind her back, and the one book he read was the New Testament. If he said something, it concerned weather or a surplus of wheat. He had a good-luck talisman, the opal-white lens of a cow's eye. Playing rummy, he rubbed it between his fingers. That soft sound and the slap of cards was about the only conversation.

Fleur finally gave them a subject.

17

Her cheeks were wide and flat, her hands large, chapped, muscular. Fleur's shoulders were broad and curved as a yoke, her hips fishlike, slippery, narrow. An old green dress clung to her waist, worn thin where she sat. Her glossy braids were like the tails of animals, and swung against her when she moved, deliberately, slowly in her work, held in and half-tamed. But only half. I could tell, but the others never noticed. They never looked into her sly brown eyes or noticed her teeth, strong and sharp and very white. Her legs were bare, and since she padded in beadworked moccasins they never saw that her fifth toes were missing. They never knew she'd drowned. They were blinded, they were stupid, they only saw her in the flesh.

And yet it wasn't just that she was a Chippewa, or even that she was a woman, it wasn't that she was good-looking or even that she was alone that made their brains hum. It was how she played cards.

Women didn't usually play with men, so the evening that Fleur drew a chair to the men's table there was a shock of surprise.

"What's this," said Lily. He was fat, with a snake's pale eyes and precious skin, smooth and lily-white, which is how he got his name. Lily had a dog, a stumpy mean little bull of a thing with a belly drum-tight from eating pork rinds. The dog was as fond of the cards as Lily, and straddled his barrel thighs through games of stud, rum poker, *vingt-un*. The dog snapped at Fleur's arm that first night, but cringed back, its snarl frozen, when she took her place.

"I thought," she said, her voice soft and stroking, "you might deal me in."

There was a space between the lead bin of spiced flour and the wall where Russell and I just fit. He tried to inch toward Fleur's skirt, to fit against her. Who knew but that he might have brought her luck like Lily's dog, except I sensed we'd be driven away if the men noticed us and so I pulled him back by the suspenders. We hunkered down, my arm around his neck. Russell smelled of caraway and pepper, of dust and sour dirt. He watched the game with tense interest for a minute or so, then went limp, leaned against me, and dropped his mouth wide. I kept my eyes open, saw Fleur's black hair swing over the chair, her feet solid on the boards of the floor. I couldn't see on the table where the cards slapped, so after they were deep in their game I pressed Russell down and raised myself in the shadows, crouched on a sill of wood.

I watched Fleur's hands stack and riffle, divide the cards, spill them to each player in a blur, rake and shuffle again. Tor, short and scrappy, shut one eye and squinted the other at Fleur. Dutch screwed his lips around a wet cigar.

"Gotta see a man," he mumbled, getting up to go out back to the privy. The others broke, left their cards, and Fleur sat alone in the lamplight that glowed in a sheen across the push of her breasts. I watched her closely, then she paid me a beam of notice for the first time. She turned, looked straight at me, and grinned the white wolf grin a Pillager turns on its victims, except that she wasn't after me.

"Pauline there," she said. "How much money you got?"

We had all been paid for the week that day. Eight cents was in my pocket.

"Stake me." She held out her long fingers. I put the coins on her palm and then I melted back to nothing, part of the walls and tables, twined close with Russell. It wasn't long before I understood something that I didn't know then. The men would not have seen me no matter what I did, how I moved. For my dress hung loose and my back was already stooped, an old woman's. Work had roughened me, reading made my eyes sore, forgetting my family had hardened my face, and scrubbing down bare boards had given me big, reddened knuckles.

When the men came back and sat around the table, they had drawn together. They shot each other small glances, stuck their tongues in their cheeks, burst out laughing at odd moments, to rattle Fleur. But she never minded. They played their *vingt-un*, staying even as Fleur slowly gained. Those pennies I had given her drew nickels and attracted dimes until there was a small pile in front of her.

Then she hooked them with five card draw, nothing wild. She dealt, discarded, drew, and then she sighed and her cards gave a little shiver. Tor's eye gleamed, and Dutch straightened in his seat.

"I'll pay to see that hand," said Lily Veddar.

Fleur showed, and she had nothing there, nothing at all.

Tor's thin smile cracked open, and he threw in his hand too.

"Well, we know one thing," he said, leaning back in his chair, "the squaw can't bluff."

With that I lowered myself into a mound of swept sawdust and slept. I woke during the night, but none of them had moved yet so I couldn't either. Still later, the men must have gone out again, or Fritzie come to break the game, because I was lifted, soothed, cradled in a woman's arms and rocked so quiet that I kept my eyes shut while Fleur rolled first me, then Russell, into a closet of grimy ledgers, oiled paper, balls of string, and thick files that fit beneath us like a mattress.

The game went on after work the next evening. Russell slept, I got my eight cents back five times over, and Fleur kept the rest of the dollar she'd won for a stake. This time they didn't play so late, but they played regular, and then kept going at it. They stuck with poker, or variations, for one solid week and each time Fleur won exactly one dollar, no more and no less, too consistent for luck.

By this time, Lily and the other men were so lit with suspense that they got Pete to join the game. They concentrated, the fat dog tense in Lily Veddar's lap, Tor suspicious, Dutch stroking his huge square brow, Pete steady. It wasn't that Fleur won that hooked them in so, because she lost hands too. It was rather that she never had a freak deal or even anything above a straight. She only took on her low cards, which didn't sit right. By chance, Fleur should have gotten a full or a flush by now. The irritating thing was she beat with pairs and never bluffed, because she couldn't, and still she ended each night with exactly one dollar. Lily couldn't believe, first of all, that a woman could be smart enough to play cards, but even if she was, that she would then be stupid enough to cheat for a dollar a night. By day I watched him turn the problem over, his lard-white face dull, small fingers probing at his knuckles, until he finally thought he had Fleur figured as a bit-time player, caution her game. Raising the stakes would throw her.

More than anything now, he wanted Fleur to come away with something but a dollar. Two bits less or ten more, the sum didn't matter just so he broke her streak.

Night after night she played, won her dollar, and left to stay in a place that only Russell and I knew about. Fritzie had done two things of value for Fleur. She had given her a black umbrella with a stout handle and material made to shed water, and also let her board on the premises. Every night, Fleur bathed in the slaughtering tub, then slept in the unused brick smokehouse behind the lockers, a windowless place tarred on the inside with scorched fats. When I brushed against her skin I noticed that she smelled of the walls, rich and woody, slightly burnt. Since that night she put me in the closet, I was no longer jealous or afraid of her, but followed her close as Russell, closer, stayed with her, became her moving shadow that the men never noticed, the shadow that could have saved her.

August, the month that bears fruit, closed around the shop and Pete and Fritzie left for Minnesota to escape the heat. A month running, Fleur had won thirty dollars and only Pete's presence had kept Lily at bay. But Pete was gone now, and one payday, with the heat so bad no one could move but Fleur, the men sat and played and waited while she finished work. The cards sweat, limp in their fingers, the table was slick with grease, and even the walls were warm to the touch. The air was motionless. Fleur was in the next room boiling heads.

Her green dress, drenched, wrapped her like a transparent sheet. A skin of lakeweed. Black snarls of veining clung to her arms. Her braids were loose, half unraveled, tied behind her neck in a thick loop. She stood in steam, turning skulls through a vat with a wooden paddle. When scraps boiled to the surface, she bent with a round tin sieve and scooped them out. She'd filled two dishpans.

"Ain't that enough now?" called Lily. "We're waiting." The stump of a dog trembled in his lap, alive with rage. It never smelled me or noticed me above Fleur's smoky skin. The air was heavy in the corner, and pressed Russell and me down. Fleur sat with the men.

"Now what do you say?" Lily asked the dog. It barked. That was the signal for the real game to start.

"Let's up the ante," said Lily, who had been stalking this night for weeks. He had a roll of money in his pocket. Fleur had five bills in her dress. Each man had saved his full pay that the bank officer had drawn from the Kozkas' account.

"Ante a dollar then," said Fleur, and pitched hers in. She lost, but they let her scrape along, a cent at a time. And then she won some. She played unevenly, as if chance were all she had. She reeled them in. The game went on. The dog was stiff now, poised on Lily's knees, a ball of vicious muscle with its yellow eyes slit in concentration. It gave advice, seemed to sniff the lay of Fleur's cards, twitched and nudged. Fleur was up, then down, saved by a scratch. Tor dealt seven cards, three down. The pot grew, round by round, until it held all the money. Nobody folded. Then it all rode on one last card and they went silent. Fleur picked hers up and drew a long breath. The heat lowered like a bell. Her card shook, but she stayed in.

Lily smiled and took the dog's head tenderly between his palms.

"Say Fatso," he said, crooning the words. "You reckon that girl's bluffing?"

The dog whined and Lily laughed. "Me too," he said. "Let's show." He tossed his bills and coins into the pot and then they turned their cards over.

Lily looked once, looked again, then he squeezed the dog like a fist of dough and slammed it on the table.

Fleur threw out her arms and swept the money close, grinning that same wolf grin that she'd used on me, the grin that had them. She jammed the bills inside her dress, scooped the coins in waxed white paper that she tied with string.

"Another round," said Lily, his voice choked with burrs. But Fleur opened her mouth and yawned, then walked out back to gather slops for the big hog that was waiting in the stockpen to be killed.

The men sat still as rocks, their hands spread on the oiled wood table. Dutch had chewed his cigar to damp shreds, Tor's eye was dull. Lily's gaze was the only one to follow Fleur. Russell and I didn't breathe. I felt them gathering, saw Dutch's veins, the ones in his forehead that stood out in anger. The dog rolled off the table and curled in a knot below the counter, where none of the men could touch him.

Lily rose and stepped to the closet of ledgers where Pete kept his private stock. He brought back a bottle, uncorked and tipped it between his fingers. The lump in his throat moved, then he passed it on. They drank, steeped in the whiskey's fire, and planned with their eyes things they couldn't say aloud.

When they left, I grabbed Russell by the arm, dragged him along. We followed, hid in the clutter of broken boards and chicken crates beside the stockpen, where the men settled. Fleur could not be seen at first, and then the moon broke and showed her, slipping cautiously along the rough board chute with a bucket in her hand. Her hair fell wild and coarse to her waist, and her dress was a floating patch in the dark. She made a pig-calling sound, rang the tin pail lightly against the wood, paused suspiciously. But too late. In the sound of the ring Lily moved, fat and nimble, stepped right behind Fleur and put out his creamy hands. Russell strained foward and I stopped his mouth with both fists before he yelled. At Lily's first touch, Fleur whirled and doused him with the bucket of sour slops. He pushed her against the big fence and the package of coins split, went clinking and jumping, winked against the wood. Fleur rolled over once and vanished into the yard.

The moon fell behind a curtain of ragged clouds, and Lily followed into the dark muck. But he tripped, pitched over the huge flank of the pig, who lay mired to the snout, heavily snoring. Russell and I sprang from the weeds and climbed the boards of the pen, stuck like glue. We saw the sow rise to her neat, knobby knees, gain her balance and sway, curious, as Lily stumbled forward. Fleur had backed into the angle of splintered wood just beyond and when Lily tried to jostle past, the sow raised her powerful neck and suddenly struck, quick and hard as a snake. She plunged at Lily's thick waist and snatched a mouthful of shirt. She lunged again, caught him lower so that he grunted in pained surprise. He seemed to ponder, breathing deep. Then he launched his huge bulk in a swimmer's dive.

The sow screamed as his body smacked over hers. She rolled, striking out with her knife-sharp hooves and Lily gathered himself upon her, took her foot-long face by the ears, and scraped her snout and cheeks against the trestles of the pen. He hurled the sow's tight skull against an iron post, but instead of knocking her dead, he woke her from her dream.

She reared, shrieked, and then he squeezed her so hard that they leaned into each other and posed in a standing embrace. They bowed jerkily, as if to begin. Then his arms swung and flailed. She sank her black fangs into his shoulder, clasping him, dancing him forward and backward through the pen. Their steps picked up pace, went wild. The two dipped as one, box-stepped, tripped one another. She ran her split foot through his hair. He grabbed her kinked tail. They went down and came up, the same shape and then the same color until the men couldn't tell one from the other in that light and Fleur was able to vault the gates, swing down, hit gravel.

The men saw, yelled, and chased her at a dead run to the smokehouse. And Lily too, once the sow gave up in disgust and freed him. That is when I should have gone to Fleur, saved her, thrown myself on Dutch the way Russell did once he unlocked my arms. He stuck to his stepfather's leg as if he'd been flung there. Dutch dragged him for a few steps, his leg a branch, then cuffed Russell off and left him shouting and bawling in the sticky weeds. I closed my eyes and put my hands on my ears, so there is nothing more to describe but what I couldn't block out: those yells from Russell, Fleur's hoarse breath, so loud it filled me, her cry in the old language and our names repeated over and over among the words.

The heat was still dense the next morning when I entered slowly through the side door of the shop. Fleur was gone and Russell slunk along the woodwork like a beaten dog. The men were slack-faced, hungover. Lily was paler and softer than ever, as if his flesh had steamed on his bones. They smoked, took pulls off a bottle. It wasn't yet noon. Russell disappeared outside to sit by the stock gate, to hold his own knees and rock back and forth. I worked awhile, waiting shop and sharpening steel. But I was sick, I was smothered, I was sweating so hard that my hands slipped on the knives and I wiped my fingers clean of the greasy touch of the customers' coins. Lily opened his mouth and roared once, not in anger. There was no meaning to the sound. His terrier dog, sprawled limp beside his foot, never lifted its head. Nor did the other men.

They didn't notice when I stepped outdoors to call Russell. And then I forgot the men because I realized that we were all balanced, ready to tip, to fly, to be crushed as soon as the weather broke. The sky was so low that I felt the weight of it like a door. Clouds hung down, witch teats, a tornado's green-brown cones, and as I watched, one flicked out and became a delicate probing thumb. Even as Russell ran to me, the wind blew suddenly, cold, and then came blinding rain.

Inside, the men had vanished and the whole place was trembling as if a huge hand was pinched at the rafters, shaking it. We ran straight through, screaming for Dutch or for any of them. Russell's fingers were clenched in my skirt. I shook him off once, but he darted after and held me close in terror when we stopped. He called for Regina, called for Fleur. The heavy doors of the lockers, where the men had surely taken shelter without us, stood shut. Russell howled. They must have heard him, even above the driving wind, because the two of us could hear, from inside, the barking of that dog. A moment, and everything went still. We didn't dare move in that strange hush of suspension. I listened, Russell too. Then we heard a cry building in the wind, faint at first, a whistle and then a shrill scream that tore through the walls and gathered around the two of us, and at last spoke plain.

It was Russell, I am sure, who first put his arms on the bar, thick iron that was made to slide along the wall and fall across the hasp and lock. He strained and shoved, too slight to move it into place, but he did not look to me for help. Sometimes, thinking back, I see my arms lift, my hands grasp, see myself dropping the beam into the metal grip. At other times, that moment is erased. But always I see Russell's face the moment after, as he turned, as he ran

27

for the door—a peaceful look of complicit satisfaction.

Then the wind plucked him. He flew as though by wires in the seat of his trousers, with me right after, toward the side wall of the shop that rose grand as a curtain, spilling us forward as the building toppled.

Outside, the wind was stronger, a hand held against us. We struggled forward. The bushes tossed, rain battered, the awning flapped off a storefront, the rails of porches rattled. The odd cloud became a fat snout that nosed along the earth and sniffed, jabbed, picked at things, sucked them up, blew them apart, rooted around as if it was following a certain scent, then stopped behind us at the butcher shop and bored down like a drill.

I pitched head over heels along the dirt drive, kept moving and tumbling in such amazement that I felt no fear, past Russell, who was lodged against a small pine. The sky was cluttered. A herd of cattle flew through the air like giant birds, dropping dung, their mouths opened in stunned bellows. A candle, still lighted, blew past, and tables, napkins, garden tools, a whole school of drifting eyeglasses, jackets on hangers, hams, a checkerboard, a lampshade, and at last the sow from behind the lockers, on the run, her hooves a blur, set free, swooping, diving, screaming as everything in Argus fell apart and got turned upside down, smashed, and thoroughly wrecked.

Days passed before the town went looking for the men. Lily was a bachelor, after all, and Tor's wife had suffered a blow to the head that made her forgetful. Understandable. But what about Regina? That would always remain a question in people's minds. For she said nothing about her husband's absence to anyone. The whole town was occupied with digging out, in high relief because even though the Catholic steeple had been ripped off like a peaked cap and sent across five fields, those huddled in the cellar were unhurt. Walls had fallen, windows were demolished, but the stores were intact and so were the bankers and shop owners who had taken refuge in their safes or beneath their cash registers. It was a fair-minded disaster, no one could be said to have suffered much more than the next, except for Kozka's Meats.

When Pete and Fritzie came home, they found that the boards of the front building had been split to kindling, piled in a huge pyramid, and the shop equipment was blasted far and wide. Pete paced off the distance the iron bathtub had been flung, a hundred feet. The glass candy case went fifty, and landed without so much as a cracked pane. There were other surprises as well, for the back rooms where Fritzie and Pete lived were undisturbed. Fritzie said the dust still coated her china figures, and upon her kitchen table, in the ashtray, perched the last cigarette she'd put out in haste. She lit and finished it, looking through the window. From there, she could see that the old smokehouse Fleur had slept in was crushed to a reddish sand and the stockpens were completely torn apart, the rails stacked helter-skelter. Fritzie asked for Fleur. People shrugged. Then she asked about the others, and suddenly, the town understood that three men were missing.

There was a rally of help, a gathering of shovels and volunteers. We passed boards from hand to hand, stacked them, uncovered what lay beneath the pile of jagged two-by-fours. The lockers, full of meat that was Pete and Fritzie's investment, slowly came into sight, still intact. When enough room was made for a man to stand on the roof, there were calls, a general urge to hack through and see what lay below. But Fritzie shouted that she wouldn't allow it because the meat would spoil. And so the work continued, board by board, until at last the solid doors of the freezer were revealed and people pressed to the entry. It was locked from the outside, someone shouted, wedged down, a tornado's freak whim. Regina stood in the crowd, clutching Russell's collar, trying to hold him against her short, tough body. Everyone wanted to be the first to enter, but only Russell and I were quick enough to slip through beside Pete and Fritzie as they shoved into the sudden icy air.

Pete scraped a match on his boot, lit the lamp Fritzie held, and then the four of us stood in its circle. Light glared off the skinned and hanging carcasses, the crates of wrapped sausages, the bright and cloudy blocks of lake ice, pure as winter. The cold bit into us, pleasant at first, then numbing. We stood there for a moment before we saw the men, or more rightly, the humps of fur, the iced and shaggy hides they wore, the bearskins they had taken down and wrapped about themselves. We stepped closer and Fritzie tilted the lantern beneath the flaps of fur into their faces. The dog was there, perched among them, heavy as a doorstop. The three had hunched around a barrel where the game was still laid out, and a dead lantern and an empty bottle too. But they had thrown down their last hands and hunkered tight, clutching one another, knuckles raw from beating at the door they had also attacked with hooks. Frost stars gleamed off their eyelashes and the stubble of their beards. Their faces were set in concentration, mouths open as if to speak some careful thought, some agreement they'd come to in each other's arms.

Only after they were taken out and laid in the sun to

thaw did someone think to determine whether they were all entirely dead, frozen solid. That is when Dutch James's faint heartbeat was discovered.

Power travels in the bloodlines, handed out before birth. It comes down through the hands, which in the Pillagers are strong and knotted, big, spidery and rough, with sensitive fingertips good at dealing cards. It comes through the eyes, too, belligerent, darkest brown, the eyes of those in the bear clan, impolite as they gaze directly at a person.

In my dreams, I look straight back at Fleur, at the men. I am no longer the watcher on the dark sill, the skinny girl.

The blood draws us back, as if it runs through a vein of earth. I left Argus, left Russell and Regina back there with Dutch. I came home and, except for talking to my cousins, live a quiet life. Fleur lives quiet too, down on Matchimanito with her boat. Some say she married the water man, Misshepeshu, or that she lives in shame with white men or windigos, or that she's killed them all. I am about the only one here who ever goes to visit her. That spring, I went to help out in her cabin when she bore the child, whose green eyes and skin the color of an old penny have made more talk, as no one can decide if the child is mixed blood or what, fathered in a smokehouse, or by a man with brass scales, or by the lake. The girl is bold, smiling in her sleep, as if she knows what people wonder, as if she hears the old men talk, turning the story over.

It comes up different every time, and has no ending, no beginning. They get the middle wrong too. They only know they don't know anything.

CHAPTER THREE

Fall 1913–Spring 1914
Onaubin-geezis
Crust on the Snow Sun

—

N A N A P U S H

Before the boundaries were set, before the sickness scattered the clans like gambling sticks, an old man never had to live alone and cook for himself, never had to braid his own hair, or listen to his silence. An old man had some relatives, got a chance to pass his name on, especially if the name was an important one like Nanapush.

My girl, listen well. Nanapush is a name that loses power every time that it is written and stored in a government file. That is why I only gave it out once in all those years.

No Name, I told Father Damien when he came to take the church census. *No Name*, I told the Agent when he made up the tribal roll.

"I have the use of a white man's name," I told the Captain

who delivered the ration payout for our first treaty, "but I won't sign your paper with that name either."

The Captain and then the lumber president, the Agent and at last many of our own, spoke long and hard about a cash agreement. But nothing changed my mind. I've seen too much go by—unturned grass below my feet, and overhead, the great white cranes flung south forever. I know this. Land is the only thing that lasts life to life. Money burns like tinder, flows off like water. And as for government promises, the wind is steadier. I am a holdout, like the Pillagers, although I told the Captain and the Agent what I thought of their papers in good English. I could have written my name, and much more too, in script. I had a Jesuit education in the halls of Saint John before I ran back to the woods and forgot all my prayers.

My father said, "Nanapush. That's what you'll be called. Because it's got to do with trickery and living in the bush. Because it's got to do with something a girl can't resist. The first Nanapush stole fire. You will steal hearts."

Not Fleur though, getting back to her. Your mother both clung to and resisted me, like any daughter. Like you're doing now.

Since I saved her from the sickness, I was entangled with her. Not that I knew it at first. Only looking back is there a pattern. I was a vine of a wild grape that twined the timbers and drew them close. Or maybe I was a branch, coming from the Kashpaws, that lived long enough to touch the next tree over, which was Pillagers, of whom there were only two—Moses and Fleur—far cousins, related not so much by blood as by name and chance survival. Or maybe there was just me, Nanapush, in the thick as ever. The name had a bearing on what happened later, as well, for it was through Fleur Pillager that the name Nanapush was carried on and won't die with me, won't rot in a case of bones and leather. There is a story to it the way there is a story to all, never visible while it is happening. Only after, when an old man sits dreaming and talking in his chair, the design springs clear.

There was so much we saw and never knew.

That fall, when Fleur walked back onto the reservation, right through town, there was not a one of us who guessed what she hid in that green rag of a dress. I do remember that it was too small, split down the back and strained across the front. Besides the black umbrella she used to shade herself, that's what I noticed when I greeted her. Not whether there was money in the dress, or a child. And who would have thought even wilder things than that—for instance that Fleur's feet, stuck bare in worn moccasins, had slid through blood? Or that she'd forced a grown man to dance with a pig? I could have rested my eyes on her for an hour, she looked that good.

"Daughter!" I said. "Come visit my place again. Tell me what you've seen."

She set her gaze on me a moment, acknowleding my sweet talk. Sometimes she called me uncle, in affection, and now she almost smiled. Then she walked on, giving nobody else a glance. She was not beaten, there was no sign of trouble. There was no way we could have known, not until Pauline returned as well, of the terrible and strange things that had happened in that white town.

But we did know that something was wrong.

The dust on the reservation stirred. Things hidden were

free to walk. The surprised young ghost of Jean Hat limped out of the bushes around the place his horse had spooked, and on the darkest nights his cart rumbled through our yards. A black dog, the form of the devil, stalked the turnoff to Matchimanito. The dog appeared to little Mrs. Bijiu and her children as they walked home from town one evening, and would not let them pass until Mrs. Bijiu thought to hold up the cross that hung around her daughter's neck. Then the dog sprang silently and horribly through the air, straight at them, but since it was *odjib,* a thing of smoke, they were unhurt. It vanished. Only the stinking odor of singed fur was left, and hung around the place, and also in their clothes, from which Mrs. Bijiu could not wash it even with lye soap.

On the other hand, the lake man retreated to the deepest rocks. The fish struck hungrily dawn and dusk, and no boats were lost. There were some who declared they were glad Fleur had come back because—we didn't like to think how she did this—she kept the lake thing controlled. But she also disturbed the area around Matchimanito. Those woods were a lonely place full of the ghosts of the drowned and those whose death took them unaware, like Jean Hat. Yet we couldn't resist hunting there. The oaks were big and the bush less dense, the berries thick and plump, the animals seemed fatter and more tender. People went there although they didn't want to meet the dead or the living, Fleur especially, or the other one either, Moses, who had defeated the sickness by turning half animal and living in a den.

In the first days of the fevers, when Moses was small, I spoke a cure for him, gave him a new name to fool death, a white name, one I'd learned from the Jesuits. I instructed his family to build a small grave house, put the food out beside it along with his clothes and possessions, and then pretend that the small boy who lived was someone else. Since they could explain none of this aloud, for fear of who might be listening, it is no wonder the child became confused. As he grew older, Moses took the charcoal from his mother's hand too often. He blackened his face and fasted for visions until he grew gaunt, but he found no answer. Perhaps he stayed too long alone in the woods, saw too much. He gained protection from the water man, the lion in the lake, and started to keep with him a litter of an old Frenchwoman's cats.

During the last disease, when he moved to the island on the far side of Matchimanito, the cats went with him. And now, whenever Moses walked into town, he wore a necklace of their claws around his neck. Though still a boy, he refused to speak to his elders even when addressed directly to his face. He stared rudely, as Pillagers had always done, and crossed his eyes at anyone who dared think Fleur's name. He came to the trading store, covered with dirt and leaves, bought Fleur's supplies and bought his own, kept them separate. We watched him fill the fur frame pack with twin bags of flour, coffee, bullets and birdshot, a twist of sugar. He bought tobacco, too, and paid for all of these things with coins and bills.

That's how everyone knew she had come back to stay. It was the money. She paid the annual fee on every Pillager allotment she had inherited, then laid in a store of supplies that would last through winter. And it was the money itself, the coins and bills, that made more talk. Before this, the Pillagers had always traded with fur, meat, hides or berries.

They never had much else. So when Moses showed in town, long arms swinging, head shaggy and low as a bison bull, clutching a leather pouch and then touching and smoothing a twenty from it, we all knew the money was from her, and that so much of it couldn't have been one summer's wages.

I waited for her to visit and tell me how.

It wasn't long before she came to my house and sat in the other chair beside the door, the place where she had once sat for a month without speaking. Even though the air was chill, I liked to sit out there and watch the road to see the design of people on their errands, to church and town, the eager step of courting boys, the secretive slide of lovers, the loads of hay that our best farmers, the Lamartines and Morrisseys, drove back and forth in poplar racks, the girls walking to the mercantile by twos, bearing cans of precious cream between them.

"Old Uncle, you're looking handsome," Fleur said when she approached.

"I don't have candy to pay your flattery," I teased.

She laughed and fiddled with my shirt collar. I used to keep peppermint in my pockets when I visited Matchimanito, in better days, other times, and she remembered. Now she looked at me quietly. Although she was carefully dressed, wrapped in her mother's beaded brown shawl, her oiled hair braided so tightly that it shone on her skull like a painted doll's, her look was tired. She leaned back, away from me, and rubbed her face.

"Daughter, are you in some kind of trouble?"

She pulled the shawl tighter and frowned at her sharp knuckles, then opened her long thin hands, turned them over, palm up, as if she would see some answer. But her fingers closed on nothing.

"I shouldn't have left this place," she said.

"Do you mean this house?" I asked, but she shook her head.

We went inside, lit the lamp, pulled chairs to the table. In my time I was known as a clever gambler. I could predict the hiding of the bones, and my years as a guide to white hunters taught me how to play cards. I had carefully guarded my one deck for years, until the paper was soft and brown, hardly stiff enough to shuffle. When Fleur pulled a fresh pack from her pocket I licked my lips.

"For you," she said, and put it on the table between us.

My hands, cold and stiff with age, warmed and grew nimble. From the piled cards I caught the fragrance of newness.

"Daughter," I said, "you have the first deal."

She insisted on cutting for the jack, which came to her on the first pass. And later, when we'd played so long it made me talkative, I said to her, "Pauline Puyat's home again."

Fleur's hands paused in shuffling. "What about it?"

"She tells a story."

Fleur smiled and her hands moved quickly.

"Uncle, the Puyat lies."

While I pondered this, I did not watch her fingers closely enough and lost and lost again to Fleur's growing amusement. But I could not cast the Puyat from my mind. You might not remember what people I'm talking about, the skinners, of whom Pauline was the only trace of those who died and scattered. She was different from the Puyats I remembered, who were always an uncertain people, shy, never leaders in our dances and cures. She was, to my mind, an unknown mixture of ingredients, like pale bannock that sagged or hardened. We never knew what to call her, or where she fit or how to think when she was around. So we tried to ignore her, and that worked as long as she was quiet. But she was different once her mouth opened and she started to wag her tongue. She was worse than a Nanapush, in fact. For while I was careful with my known facts, she was given to improving truth.

Because she was unnoticeable, homely if it must be said, Pauline schemed to gain attention by telling odd tales that created damage. There was some question if she wasn't afflicted, touched in the mind. Her Aunt Regina, who was married to a Dutchman, sent the girl back here when she got peculiar, blacked out and couldn't sleep, saw things that weren't in the room. That is all to say that the only people who believed Pauline's stories were the ones who loved the dirt. But of those there are no shortage.

People speculated.

They added up the money and how they never saw Fleur, and came out betting there would be a baby in the woods. Someone in the town could have paid Fleur Pillager that money to leave and never come around again. She could even have stolen it from the man. Everybody thought they would know for sure, in nine months or fewer, and then young Eli Kashpaw stepped in and muddied the waters.

This Eli was not much like his father, or even his younger brother Nector, in that he never cared to figure out business, politics, or church. He never applied for a chunk of land or registered himself, while Nector did both, and also learned to write while he was no more than a child. Eli never held a pen in his hand. Nector wrote letters after five winters, each word formed as perfectly as the nuns shaped theirs.

Eli hid from authorities, never saw the inside of a classroom, and although his mother, Margaret (Rushes Bear, she later called herself, once she began to run things around here in earnest), got baptized in the church and tried to collar him for Mass, the best he did was sit outside the big pine door and whittle pegs. Nector, on the other hand, served Mass for Father Damien.

For money, Eli chopped wood, pitched hay, harvested potatoes or cranberry bark. He wanted to be a hunter, though, like me, and asked to partner that winter before the sickness.

I think like animals, have perfect understanding for where they hide, and in my time I have tracked a deer back through time and brush and cleared field, to the place it was born. You smile! There was only one thing wrong with teaching these important things, however. I showed Eli how to hunt and trap from such an early age that I think he lived too much in the company of trees and wind. At fifteen, he was uncomfortable around humans, especially women.

His eyes skittered and his hands twisted in his pockets when they came around. He could not stand quiet long enough for a girl to notice he was not bad-looking, a slim boy with eyebrows bent over his long nose. But then, even if she noticed, Eli could not so much as greet her without breaking into a sweat and choking out a foolish, slow apology. For a while, some thought the greater balance of the brains and Kashpaw shrewd-mindedness went to Nector, although that boy was born last and they say the final child is made of poorer stuff.

Eli was just quieter, more thoughtful, slower in his actions and conclusions. I knew this. For it turned out Eli knew how to land on his feet, how to let his shy ignorance work in his favor. Those foolish mistakes that he made later on resulted from desperation, but he did have charm, invisible to me but obvious, in some way, to Fleur. How else, in the beginning, could he have figured out a way of surviving her?

Of course, I helped him out.

I'm Nanapush, remember. That's as good as saying I knew what interested Eli Kashpaw. He wanted something other than what I could teach him about the woods. He was no longer curious only about where a mink will fish or burrow, or when pike lie low or bite. He wanted to hear how, in the days before the priest's ban and the sickness, I satisfied three wives.

"Nanapush," said Eli, appearing at my door one day. "I have to ask you something."

"Come in here then," I said. "I won't bite you like the little girls."

He was steadier, more serious than last winter when we'd gone out together on the trapline. I was going to wonder what the different thing about him was when he said, "Fleur Pillager."

"She's no little girl," I answered, motioning toward the table. He told me the story.

It began when Eli got himself good and lost up near Matchimanito. He was hunting a doe in a light rain, having no luck, until he rounded a slough and shot badly, which wasn't unusual. She was wounded to death but not crippled. She might walk all day, which shamed him, so he dabbed a bit of her blood on the barrel of his gun, the charm I taught him, and he followed her trail.

He had a time of it. She sawed through the woods, took the worst way, moved into heavy brush like a ghost. For hours, Eli blazed his passage with snapped branches and clumps of leaves, scuffed the ground or left a bootprint. But the trail and the day wore on. For some reason that he did not understand, he gave up and quit leaving sign.

"That was when you should have turned back," I told him. "You should have known. It's no accident people don't like to go there. Those trees are too big, thick and twisted at the top like bent arms. In the wind their limbs cast, creak against each other, snap. The leaves speak a cold language that overfills your brain. You want to lie down. You want to never get up. You hunger. You rake black chokecherries off their stems and stuff them down you, then you shit like a bird. Your blood thins. You're too close to where the lake man lives. And you're too close to where I buried the Pillagers during the long sickness that claimed them like it claimed the Nanapush clan."

I said this to Eli Kashpaw, "I understand Fleur. I am alone. I know that was no ordinary doe drawing you out there."

But the doe was real enough, he told me, gutshot and weakening. The blood dropped fresher, darker, until he thought he heard her just ahead and bent to the ground, desperate to see in the falling dusk, and looked ahead to catch a glimpse, and instead saw the glow of fire. He started toward it, stopped just outside the circle of light. The deer hung, already split, turning back and forth on a rope. When he saw the woman gutting with long quick movements, arms bloody and bare, he stepped into the clearing.

"That's mine," he said.

I hid my face, shook my head.

"You should have turned back," I told him. "Stupid! You should have left it."

But he was stubborn, a vein of Kashpaw that held out for what it had coming. He couldn't have taken the carcass home anyway, couldn't have lugged it back, even if he had known his direction. Yet he stood his ground with the woman, and said he'd tracked that deer too far to let it go. She did not respond. "Or maybe half," he thought, studying her back, uncomfortable. Even so, that was as generous as he could get.

She kept working. Never noticed him. He was so ignorant that he reached out and tapped her on the shoulder. She never even twitched. He walked around her, watched the knife cut, trespassed into her line of vision.

At last she saw him, he said, but then scorned him as though he were nothing.

"Little fly." She straightened her back, the knife loose and casual in her hand. "Quit buzzing."

Eli said she looked so wild her beauty didn't throw him, and I leaned closer, worried as he said this, worried as he reported how her hair was clumped with dirt, her face thin as a bony bitch, her dress a rag that hung and no curve to her except her breasts.

He noticed some things.

"No curve?" I said, thinking of the rumors.

He shook his head, impatient to continue his story. He felt sorry for her, he said. I told him the last man that pitied Fleur was found feet up in his bathtub, drowned. I was a friend to the Pillagers before they died off, I said, and I was safe from Fleur because the two of us had mourned the dead together. She was almost a relative. But that wasn't the case with him.

Eli looked at me with an unbelieving frown. Then he

said he didn't see where she was so dangerous. After a while, he recognized her manner as exhaustion more than anger. She made no protest when he took out his own knife and helped her work. Halfway through the job, she allowed him to finish alone, and then Eli hoisted most of the meat into the tree. He took the choice parts into the cabin. She let him in, hardly noticed him, and he helped her start the small range and even took it on himself to melt lard. She ate the whole heart, fell on it like a starved animal, then her eyes shut.

From the way he described her actions, I was sure she was pregnant. I'm familiar with the signs, and I can talk about this since I'm an old man far past anything a woman can do to weaken me. I was more certain still when Eli said that he took her in his arms, helped her to a pile of blankets on a willow bed. And then this, hard for an old man to believe even though it was, for the first time, the right thing to do, Eli rolled in a coat the other side of the cabin floor and lay there all night, and slept alone.

"So," I said, "why have you come to me now? You got away, you survived, she even let you find your way back home. You learned your lesson and none the worse."

"I want her," Eli said.

I could not believe that I heard right, but we were sitting by the stove, face to face, so there was no doubt. I rose and turned my back. Maybe I was less than generous, having lost my own girls. Maybe I wanted to keep Fleur as my daughter, who would visit me, joke with me, beat me at cards. But I believe it was only for Eli's own good that I was harsh.

"Forget that thing so heavy in your pocket," I said, "or

put it somewhere else. Go town way and find yourself a tamed woman."

He brooded at my tabletop, then spoke. "I want know-how, not warnings, not my mother's caution."

"You don't want instruction!" I was pushed too far. "Love medicine is what you're after. A Nanapush never needed any, but old lady Aintapi or the Pillagers, they sell it. Go ask Moses for a medicine and pay your price."

"I don't want anything that can wear off," the boy said. He was determined. Maybe his new, steady coolness was the thing that turned my mind, the quiet of him. He was different, sitting there so still. It struck me that he had come into his growth, and who was I to hold him back from going to a Pillager, since someone had to, since the whole tribe had got to thinking that she couldn't be left alone out there, a woman gone wild, striking down whatever got into her path. People said that she had to be harnessed. Maybe, I thought, Eli was the young man to do it, even though he couldn't rub two words together and get a spark.

So I gave in. I told him what he wanted to know. He asked me the old-time way to make a woman love him and I went into detail so he should make no disgraceful error. I told him about the first woman who had given herself to me. Sanawashonekek, her name was, the Lying Down Grass, the place where a deer has spent the night. I described the finicky taste of Omiimii, the Dove, and the trials I'd gone through to keep my second wife pleasured. Zezikaaikwe, the Unexpected, was a woman whose name was the exact prediction of her desires. I gave him a few things from the French trunk my third wife left, but I wasn't ready yet to speak of White Beads, or the daughter we had together, nicknamed Lulu. I showed a white woman's fan, bead leggings, a little girl's soft doll made of fawn skin.

When Eli Kashpaw stroked their beauty and asked where these things had come from, I remembered the old days. Talk is an old man's last vice. I opened my mouth and wore out the boy's ears, but that is not my fault. I shouldn't have been caused to live so long, shown so much of death, had to squeeze so many stories in the corners of my brain. They're all attached, and once I start there is no end to telling because they're hooked from one side to the other, mouth to tail. During the year of sickness, when I was the last one left, I saved myself by starting a story. One night I was ready to bring to the other side the doll I now gave Eli. My wife had sewed it together after our daughter died and I held it in my hands when I fainted, lost breath, so that I could hardly keep moving my lips. But I did continue and recovered. I got well by talking. Death could not get a word in edgewise, grew discouraged, and traveled on.

Eli returned to Fleur, and stopped badgering me, which I took as a sign she liked the fan, the bead leggings, and maybe the rest of Eli, the part where he was on his own. The thing I've found about women is that you must use every instinct to confuse.

"Look here," I told Eli before he went out my door, "it's like you're a log in a stream. Along comes this bear. She jumps on. Don't let her dig in her claws."

So keeping Fleur off balance was what I presumed Eli was doing. But as it turned out he was farther along than that, way off and running beyond reach of anything I said.

His mother was the one who gave me the news.

Margaret Kashpaw was a woman who had sunk her claws in the log and peeled it to a toothpick, and she wasn't going to let any man forget it. Especially me, her dead husband's partner in some youthful pursuits.

"Aneesh," she said, slamming my door shut. There was no knocking with Margaret because with warning you might get your breath, or escape. She was headlong, bossy, scared of nobody and full of vinegar. She was a little woman, but so blinded by irritation that she'd take on anyone. She was thin on the top and plump as a turnip below, with a face like a round molasses cake. On each side of it gray plaits hung. With age, her part had widened down the middle so it looked as though the braids were slipping off her head. Her eyes were harsh, bright, and her tongue honed keen. She sat right down.

"Would you care to know what you have my son doing?"

I mumbled, kept reading by the window, tucked my spectacles from Father Damien more comfortably around my ears. My newspaper came from Grand Forks once a week. There was bad news from overseas, and I wasn't about to let Margaret spoil my concentration or get past my hiding place.

"Which son?" I said. "Eli's little shadow? You mean Nector?"

"Sah!" She swiped at the sheets with her hand, grazed the print, but never quite dared to flip it aside. This was not for any fear of me, however. She didn't want the tracks rubbing off on her skin. She never learned to read, and the mystery troubled her.

I took advantage of that, snapped the paper in front of

my face and sat for a moment. But she won, of course, because she knew I'd get curious. I felt her eyes glittering beyond the paper, and when I put the pages down she continued.

"Who learned my Eli to make love standing up! Who learned him to have a woman against a tree in clear daylight? Who learned him to..."

"Wait," I said, "how'd you get to know this?"

She shrugged it off, then said in a smaller voice, "Boy Lazarre."

And I, who knew that the dirty Lazarres don't spy for nothing, just smiled.

"How much did you pay the fat-bellied dog?"

"They're like animals in their season! No sense of shame!" But the wind was out of her. "Against the wall of the cabin," she said, "down beside it. In grass and up in trees. Who'd he learn that from?"

"Maybe my late partner Kashpaw," I pondered.

She puffed her cheeks out, fumed. "Not from him!"

"Not that you knew." I put my spectacles carefully upon the windowsill. Her hand could snake out quickly.

She hissed. The words flew like razor grass between her teeth.

"Old man," she scorned, "two wrinkled berries and a twig."

"A twig can grow," I offered.

"But only in the spring."

Then she was gone, out the door, leaving my tongue tingling for the last word, and still ignorant of the full effect of my advice. It didn't occur to me till later to wonder if it didn't go both ways, though, if Fleur had wound her private hairs around the buttons of Eli's shirt, if she had stirred smoky powders or crushed snakeroot into his tea. Perhaps she had bitten his nails in sleep, swallowed the ends, snipped threads from his clothing and made a doll to wear between her legs.

For they got bolder, until the whole reservation gossiped.

Then one day the big unsteady Lazarre, an Indian whose birth certificate was recorded simply "Boy," returned from the woods talking backwards, garbled, mixing his words. At first people thought the sights of passion had cleft his mind. Then they figured otherwise, imagined that Fleur had caught Lazarre watching and tied him up, cut his tongue out, then sewn it in reversed.

The same day I heard this, Margaret burst into my house a second time.

"Take me out to their place, you four-eyes," she ordered.

"And I want to go the short way, across the lake. So be ready with the boat tomorrow, sunup," was her parting shot. She stamped through the door and vanished, leaving me with hardly time enough to patch the seams and holes of the old-time boat I kept, dragged up in a brush shelter on the quieter inlet, the south end of the lake. I took some boiled pine gum to the seams that afternoon, and did my best. I was drawn to the situation, curious myself, and though I didn't want to spy either on the girl whose life I'd saved, or the boy I'd advised on courting, I was down by the water with the paddles at dawn.

The light was chill and green, the waves on the lake were small confused ripples and no steady wind had gathered. We left young Nector pouting on shore, but safe. The water could be deceptive, set snares for the careless young or for withered-up and eager fools like ourselves. I put my hand in the current.

"Margaret," I said, "the lake's too cold. I never could swim, either, not that good."

But Margaret had set her mind, and made her peace too.

"If he wants me"—she was talking about the lake man but, out of caution, using no names—"I'll give him good as I get."

"Oh," I said, "has it been that long, Margaret?"

Her eyes lit and I wished I had kept my mouth shut. But she only commented, later, after we had launched, "Not so long as I would consider the dregs." I handed her the lard can I kept my bait in.

"You better take this, Margaret. You better bail."

So at least on that long trip across I had the satisfaction of seeing her bend to the dipping and pouring with a sour but desperate will. We rode low. The water covered our ankles by the time we beached on shore, but Margaret was forced to shut her mouth in a firm line. The whole idea had been hers. She was so relieved to finally stand upon solid ground that she helped me haul the boat and wedge it between a pile of mangled roots. She wrung her skirt, sat beside me, panting with our efforts. She shared out some dried meat from the pocket of her dress, tore at it like a young snapping turtle. How I envied her sharp, strong teeth.

"Go on, eat," she said, "or I'll take an insult."

I put the jerky into my mouth.

"That's right," she sneered, "suck long enough and it will soften."

I had no choice. There was no other way to get any of it down.

"Go now," I said after a while. "I was thinking. I had this old barren she-dog once. She'd back up to anything. But the only satisfaction she could get was from watching the young."

Margaret jumped to her feet, skirts flapping. I had said too much. Her claws gave my ears two fast furious jerks that set me whirling, sickened me so that I couldn't balance straight or even keep track of time. She took herself up the bank and into the Pillager woods, but I don't know when she went there, how long she stayed, and had barely set myself to rights before she returned.

By then the sky had gone dead gray, the waves rolled white and fitful. Margaret pinched tobacco from a pouch in her pocket, threw it on the water and said a few distracted, imploring words. We jumped into the boat, which leaked worse than ever, and pushed off. The wind blew harsh, in heavy circular gusts, and I was hard put. I never saw the bailing can move so fast, before or since. The old woman made it flash and dip, and hardly even broke the rhythm halfway across when she reached into her pocket again and this time dumped the whole pouch into the pounding waves. From then on she alternated, between the working of her arms, addressing different Manitous along with the Blessed Virgin and Her heart, the sacred bloody lump that the blue-robed woman held in the awful picture Margaret kept nailed to her wall. We made it back by the time the rain poured down, and hoisted ourselves over the edge of the boat. When we got back to my house, I stirred the fire and after she'd swallowed some warm broth and her clothes had begun to steam dry upon her, Margaret told me what she had seen with her own eyes.

Fleur Pillager was pregnant, going to have a child in spring. At least that's what Margaret had decided with her measuring gaze.

So now Margaret had to work fast. She was desperate to get her son back. To this end, she made her last stab, her last-ditch attempt, and it was a good one. So good it almost worked.

Margaret Kashpaw went underground for dirt.

While Eli set a trapline around the Pillagers' lake and went out to check it, for weeks on end now, without his little brother, Margaret set her own trapline, too. Hers was just as carefully laid out, around the kitchen table. She placed dishes, cups, coffee and new gaulette, grease and dried berries, bait for whoever might come. Sooner or later, she knew, someone would. And they did, although it took until after snow lay deep.

One afternoon, in a thaw of midwinter, Pauline took the lure. I happened to be visiting the table too, stealing food like a weasel, listening with open ears. Naturally, once Pauline's mouth started it couldn't stop. It was as if she took the first drink, and from then on the drinks took her. She sat in Margaret's chair. She was a quick and brittle thing, all nerves, and she stuffed bread down and babbled through the crumbs. As her lips moved, her eyes skimmed from wall to floor, never meeting anyone's glance, so anxious to be believed. Her brown hair poked in straggles around her ears. Her hands shook like ragged wings when her voice went high.

She'd known Fleur, she said, she'd worked with her in Argus. Pauline pursed her mouth and frowned, then continued. There was the butcher shop, the cards, what happened in the smokehouse. In describing the things she had not seen her fingers wandered in the air, her voice screeched. We said nothing, only stared as if she were a talking bird. As I have said, she was born a liar, and sure to die one. The practice of deception was so constant with her that it got to be a kind of truth.

"Go on," I said, "the only thing we know for sure is Fleur Pillager had money in her dress. No crime in that."

"How she got it, though!" Margaret said.

Pauline guzzled coffee, played with the cross around her neck and looked sorry and surprised at her own thoughts.

"The jealous hens like to squawk," I said, downing a ladle of thick berry pudding before Margaret snatched the bowl from my hands.

"Some men just come over here to stuff themselves."

"I'm leaving," I said, "right now. I'm leaving you empty bowls." By the way I said it, they knew the insult I intended. Margaret's eyes took fire and Pauline's color deepened and blotched.

"In the old days," said Margaret quickly, "even the white-haired ones could do more than talk."

"You should see me in the morning," I boasted.

Pauline's eyes went huge and she shifted in her chair. Margaret could not resist temptation.

"You'll die hard," Margaret pretended to scold. "You'll stick up through the dirt."

Pauline screamed, crammed the corner of her apron into her mouth and ran out the door. By then, Margaret didn't care. She had the story of Fleur and Argus, in the words of a firsthand witness.

I went away. A man needs no reminding of his mortality,

and Pauline had recently become a helper to Bernadette— the one who washed and laid out our dead. Sometimes, now, Pauline sat the death watch too. She might look after a widower's children for the first night, might bake and cook for a dead man's funeral, gloat in the church while the priest read. She was the crow of the reservation, she lived off our scraps, and she knew us best because the scraps told our story.

I didn't want Pauline ever to know me in death. Not with those cold eyes, light and curious, sharp pins. I'd go off in the bush like a sick dog first, alone.

For days after their conversation, Margaret cleaned and swept with new vigor. It was right for the girl to get this out into the open, she told me. Knowledge kept in could kill a person like Pauline.

Margaret spoke with the satisfaction of one who benefits from her own generosity, although it was true enough. No one who saw Pauline afterwards could doubt the good it did her to be set free of the tale. She walked lighter, as if the story had weighed on her before. People said that coming back from Communion, with the host held in her mouth, she was smug with the relief of her innocence. For now the burden of her secret was passed to Margaret.

Only Margaret didn't see it as a burden, but rather as a blessing that took her like a thunderclap between the eyes, thrilling her so completely that she didn't know, at first, how to use it. For a while, she simply studied the puzzle. In her mind and counting back, it was soon for the child to show, but not impossible. Fleur had been home on the reservation one month before attracting Eli, which she did with the charm she wore between her legs, said Margaret, because she needed a husband. Margaret was certain the child was not fathered by Eli, but she would have to wait until the day it arrived for the total proof. It would turn out cleft, she predicted, fork-footed like a pig, with straw for hair. Its eyes would glow blue, its skin shine dead white. Margaret savored the variations the child might reveal. Red flapping ears, a strange birthmark, chicken lips, an extra finger, by which the taint of its conception would be certain. Pauline's story gave her other ammunition. Fleur had enticed the men to her and then killed them for her amusement. Wasn't a rumor like this enough to warn off any man?

Margaret believed so, and some of the others did too, although for me I not only considered Fleur a daughter, but understood from a man's point of view that the danger might not matter, given how Fleur looked and acted, so impossible and yet available at the same time, that even the dried-out and bent ones around the store could see enough to light a slow fuse in their dreams.

To my mind anyway, there wasn't much a woman could say to her son once he had made up his mind. But Margaret Kashpaw had another view, a confidence no one could shake, in her ability always to draw her boy back into her arms. Some mothers swell up on the power of giving life, so much that they harbor the notion they can shrink their children back to seeds. Margaret was one of those.

Along into the winter, I was visiting Margaret when skinny Nector, who we teased was Eli's twin because he so imitated and resembled his older brother, came through the door with a heron. The bird was gray, alive, with yellow luminous eyes and a crippled wing. Nector set it down and tied its scaly feet with a strip of rag, then the wings too. He wound the cloth around and around the bird, trussing it completely, so that only its head could move. After the stunned terror wore off it thrust with its snake-neck, jabbed the air. Its wing had been long hurt so it couldn't fly south, and how it had lived through the first part of the winter, on what, we had no notion.

Eli came in, put his hand on his brother's shoulders, and Nector said he'd gone and caught the bird for Eli's wife.

"Wife!" said Margaret, but it was clear she'd heard this word before. "No wife of yours will ever live on any land but Kashpaws'. You'll bring her home." Of course, she knew there was no chance of this with Fleur. She never flinched, just grabbed the bird's beak and held it still.

Eli paid no attention to that. He said to Nector, "She likes birds."

"She likes all types of animals," said Margaret in a challenging way.

The heron glared from the middle of the table, Margaret's hand on the beak. At Eli's laugh, she set her puckered face and pouting lips and forgot I was listening.

Margaret's voice trembled, but as she looked at her older son, her eyes were hard as birdshot. "I guess you'll be leaving us to fend for ourselves," she said with deceptive meekness.

Eli's look said that he would not take the bait she dropped, and argue. His path was obvious. His hair was growing from the barbershop cut Margaret had given him, creeping down his neck and over his collar. He looked young, flushed and gleaming, on fire. All week he had been on the trapline with Fleur and he might as well have been in the next world, or the one before, for all he cared of this one now.

"I'm good as married, Mama," was all he had to say to cause Margaret's hand to move, unleashing the heron as she spoke, riveting Eli's attention with her voice so that he couldn't react quickly enough when it reached for his hand

and speared it like a frog. The two began to shout and accuse each other in the most eager way, then, so I grabbed the bird, tied its beak with a bit of cloth, and left with Nector at my side.

You might have thought that by now the old woman would have given in, but the truth is she couldn't then and she never really did. Since her older children were all gone, moved to their allotment land in Montana, she wanted a place right here that she could trust for her old age. Eli was her best chance. She couldn't rely on Nector, whose love of town ways seemed to head him so clearly for the off-reservation schools. She wanted a simpleminded daughter-in-law she could boss, a girl who would take advice and not bar her from the house. Everyone knew Fleur Pillager wasn't like that, did not need a second mother. Ogimaakwe had raised her daughters to boss themselves. Or so Margaret thought until Pauline came knocking, months later, when Fleur's child was finally ready to be born.

This is where you come in, my girl, so listen.

It was spring by then, the ice milky, porous and broken, the water open for a boat if you dared to travel that way, which I did. Fleur was in trouble with her baby. That's all I heard, as Pauline and Margaret kept the particulars to themselves. Not knowing any better, Eli had brought Pauline to help, but she was useless—good at easing souls into death but bad at breathing them to life, afraid of life in fact, afraid of birth, and afraid of Fleur Pillager. So the girl fetched Margaret, who might, after all, be the grandmother.

We took the quick way again, paddling across. Several times on the ride, bailing for her life, Margaret scolded me for keeping my boat in such poor condition. She assured me repeatedly that her reasons for helping in this matter were not ties of kinship. Her presence did not count as acknowledgment, but it was her duty to see the evidence, whatever that turned out to be—the hair of gold straw, the blazing eyes.

But you had none of those markings.

You were born on the day we shot the last bear, drunk, on the reservation. Pauline was the one who shot it, and the bear was drunk, not her. That she-bear had broken into the trader's wine I had brought across the lake beneath my jacket and then stowed in a rotten stump off in the woods behind the house. She bit the cork and emptied the white clay jug, then lost her mind and stumbled into the beaten grass of Fleur's yard.

By then we were a day in the waiting, with Nector left at Margaret's to shift for himself. All that time there was no sound from Fleur's cabin, just crushing silence like the inside of a drum before the stick drops. Eli and I slumped against the woodpile. We made a fire, swaddled ourselves in blankets. My stomach creaked with the lack of food, for Eli was starving himself from worry and I hated to eat in front of him. His eyes were rimmed with blood as he moaned and talked and prayed beneath the burden, which grew heavier.

On the second day, we leaned to the fire, strained for the sound of the cry a baby makes. Our ears picked up everything in the woods, the rustle of birds, the crack of dead spring leaves and twigs. Our hearing had by then grown so keen that we heard the muffled sound the women made inside the house. Now there was more activity, which gave us hope. The stove lid clanked, pans rang together. Pauline or Margaret came to the door and we heard the tear of water splashing on the ground. Eli moved then, fetched more. But it wasn't until the afternoon of that second day that the stillness finally broke, and then, it was as if the Manitous all through the woods spoke through Fleur, loose, arguing. I recognized them. Turtle's quavering scratch, the Eagle's high shriek, Loon's crazy bitterness, Otter, the howl of Wolf, Bear's low rasp.

Perhaps the bear heard Fleur calling, and answered.

I was alone when it happened, since Eli had broken when the silence shattered, slashed his arm with his hunting knife, and run out of the clearing, straight north. I sat quietly after he was gone, and sampled the food that he had refused. I drew close to the fire, settled my back against the split logs, and was just about to have a second helping when the drunk bear rambled past. She sniffed the ground, rolled over in an odor that pleased her, drew up and sat, addled, on her haunches like a dog. I jumped straight onto the top of the woodpile, I don't know how, since my limbs were so stiff from the wet cold. I crouched, yelled at the house, screamed for the gun, but only attracted the bear. She dragged herself over, gave a drawn-out whine, a cough, and fixed me with a long, patient stare.

Margaret flung the door open. "Shoot it, you old fool," she hollered. But I was empty-handed. Margaret was irritated with this trifle, put out that I had not obeyed her, anxious to get rid of the nuisance and go back to Fleur. She marched straight toward us. Her face was pinched with exhaustion, her pace furious. Her arms moved like pistons and she came so fast that she and the bear were face to face before she realized that she had nothing with which to attack. She was sensible, Margaret Kashpaw, and turned straight around. Fleur kept her gun above the flour cupboard in a rack of antlers, but Margaret never reached it. The bear followed, heeling her like a puppy, and at the door to the house, when Margaret turned, arms spread to bar the way, it swatted her aside with one sharp dreamy blow. Then it ambled in and reared on its hind legs.

I am a man, so I don't know exactly what happened when the bear came into the birth house, but they talk among themselves, the women, and sometimes they forget I'm listening. So I know that when Fleur saw the bear in the house she was filled with such fear and power that she raised herself on the mound of blankets and gave birth. Then Pauline took down the gun and shot point-blank, filling the bear's heart. She says so anyway. But she says that the lead only gave the bear strength, and I'll support that. For I heard the gun go off and then saw the creature whirl and roar from the house. It barreled past me, crashed through the brush into the woods, and was not seen after. It left no trail either, so it could have been a spirit bear. I don't know. I was still on the woodpile.

I took the precaution of finishing my meal there. From what I overheard later, they were sure Fleur was dead, she was so cold and still after giving birth. But then the baby cried. That, I heard with my own ears. At that sound, they say, Fleur opened her eyes and breathed. That was when Margaret went to work and saved her, packed wormwood and moss between her legs, wrapped her in blankets heated with stones, then kneaded Fleur's stomach and forced her to drink cup after cup of boiled raspberry leaf until at last Fleur groaned, drew the baby against her breast, and lived.

And now you ask how you got to be a Nanapush. You wonder how a man with no wife got his name extended.

Well of course, it was through the custom by which we obliged our friend Father Damien, that of baptism. I was still there the next day when the priest came, prepared for the last rites but very pleased to have a new life in their place. He carried his host and chalice. I gave him a dipper from the bucket. He greeted Margaret, but sensed the correct way, and did not cross the threshold.

Margaret whispered so as not to awaken Fleur. She let the priest pour blessed water on the baby's head and say the words, but hearing Fleur, she snatched the child indoors before it could be named. I was left with Damien by the woodpile, where by then I had built a small brush shelter.

"I must complete the records," he said. "The father's name?"

I didn't speak immediately, but thought about his question first. I persuaded myself that Eli might not come back, and then even if he did, who knew for certain about his being the father? Besides, he was young, and with brothers to help him there would always be descendants in his clan. I thought how Margaret had jeered at my abilities. I thought about the afternoon Pauline ran her mouth. I thought about my wives, especially White Beads and our daughter. I had the opportunity to speak now, and the right. I had kept a good blaze going for the women in the cabin by splitting wood until I thought the stringy muscles in my arms would burst. There were so many tales, so many possibilities, so many lies. The waters were so muddy I thought I'd give them another stir.

"Nanapush," I said. "And her name is Lulu."

Winter 1914–Summer 1917
Meen-geezis
Blueberry Sun

—

P A U L I N E

Ileft Argus because I couldn't get rid of the men. They walked nightlong through my dreams, looking for whom to blame. Pauline! My name was a growl on their lips. A suspicion, a certainty, an iron hook on a rail.

Dutch James rotted in the bedroom, sawed away piece by piece. First the doctor took one leg mostly off, then the other foot, an arm up to the elbow. His ears wilted off his head. He was kept dosed with morphine and he sometimes talked long into the night. Regina, in the chair with her bark and her quills and her embroidery, answered him, soothed him, told him long tales. That was a strange thing. All of a sudden, she loved him and he loved her. I could sense it naked in his eyes, in the hum of her voice, the gentle whispers between them. It was a horrible kind of honeymoon: bedpans and stinking bandages of rolled white cotton, boiled shears, hateful airlessness, windows that could not be opened for the flies.

Yet Regina would surely make him well. And because even well he would be helplessly bound to her, Regina took an interest in him now and cared for him like a child. She didn't need me anymore. I was just as anxious to get free. Dutch embarrassed me. To the house on the margins of town, he drew a stream of church auxiliary women, each one laden. They could be counted on to bring a torte or flummery, a chicken cut to pieces and cooked pale, a pot of saw beans, a rice ring green with spinach or chard, any one of these the admission price to gaze on Dutch.

He was a wonder, and the food piled around us as he decreased. On seeing him, the ladies' mouths dropped, their breath came fast. They pulled white squares of cambric from their sleeve ends and touched the scented cloth to their noses. Their eyes watered. When at last the air had turned freezing cold and we could keep the pans and pies locked in a shed, when at last those visits ended, Dutch healed over enough to marry my aunt. It was December, dry, the roads still clear, when I finally saw my chance.

The widow Bernadette Morrissey and her brother Napoleon came down to Argus one day in a fine green wagon. Both of them were swaddled in sheepskin coats, warm and heavy. They came to trade for things that couldn't be got up north on the reservation. They were well-off people, mixed-bloods who profited from acquiring allotments that many old Chippewa did not know how to keep. The farm was big for those days, six hundred and forty acres. Even though Napoleon had a weakness for drink, even though he was a bachelor, confirmed to it as if tapped by the bishop, he was considered a good Catholic and a dutiful brother to take in his sister and her three children. Bernadette's big handsome son, Clarence, had helped build a two-story house. They kept chickens, a barn with six cows for milking, two pigs, a kitchen garden, and even some geese. Bernadette's two other children were daughters, Sophie and Philomena. Sophie was the older, tall and messy. Philomena was sweet and fat. I knew them from before, from the nun's school, and though I'd hated their pretty and assured French ways then, I counseled myself to ask after them, to yearn after them, to lower my eyes and stare at my feet in confusion until Bernadette asked what was wrong. Then I told her.

How I was beaten by Regina. Cursed by Dutch. Mocked by my small cousin Russell, whom I did not want to leave behind, but must. I told how I scrubbed the rough boards and clabbered milk, boiled salves and washed bandages, how homesick I had become.

"The work will be no easier with us," said Bernadette, "but we will not beat you."

Bernadette had known my mother, and disapproved of the way I had been left behind. She offered pure charity, but I accepted. I would not have false pride and obstruct the reward that Bernadette would eventually receive from God.

Besides, I do believe I was kin to Bernadette Morrissey. We looked so alike coming down the road, stark and bony as starved cows, and I was similar in mind, much more so than her own daughters. Bernadette was the one who taught me how to read and write the nun's script that she'd learned, French educated in Quebec. She had a whole trunk full of pamphlets and books and knew numbers, kept the accounts for the farm, always took a sheet of figures along when she went to visit the sick and dying. In the deep night, waiting for the angel's wings to fold, she totaled and divided and subtracted and found amounts. The nuns thought her holy because she visited the dead. I knew she was practical and needed quiet to balance books.

As for Napoleon, I will not say that I encouraged the attentions he soon paid. I pretended not to notice where his hand dropped, his elbow brushed. I shied from sitting near him or jigging for him barefoot when he played the fiddle. I knew Bernadette would surely send me back if he got bolder, unless he offered more. Girls my age married, it is true. But not usually to men so gray and lined with the marks of hard fortune and distilled drink. He was as old as the men at the shop, and even fonder of the bottle. He hid his whiskey in the mangers, in the corn crib, buried it under rocks in the woods, offered it to me.

"Pour it out," I whispered, cornered behind the house. He put the belly of the jar to my cheek, rolled it back and forth, laughing at me standing so rigid and afraid.

At least the dreams stopped once Argus was behind me, that is, until I made the mistake of talking aloud and bringing the whole of what had happened back to life. It was because of Margaret Kashpaw's scheming. She pulled the truth or some version of it out of me, I don't know how, then despised me because I was too weak to resist her. When I left the Kashpaw house, I felt both heavier and lighter. I was lighter because I had unburdened my shoulders, and heavier because I knew the dreams would fall.

And they did, only now I dreamed particularly of Fleur. Not as she was on the reservation, living in the woods, but of those last days, of the lockers where I was broken by her, pressed by her, driven like a leaf in wind. I relived the whole thing over and over, that moment so clear before the storm. Every night when my arms lowered the beam, it was my will that bore the weight, let it drop into place—not Russell's and not Fleur's. For that reason, at the Judgment, it would be my soul sacrificed, my poor body turned on the devil's wheel. And yet, despite that future, I was condemned to suffer in this life also. Every night I was witness when the men slapped Fleur's mouth, beat her, entered and rode her. I felt all. My shrieks poured from her mouth and my blood from her wounds.

I grew afraid to shut my eyes, knowing I would thrash in my sleep and kick Sophie and Philomena, who shared the bed. But I always did sleep, dream, and through the weeks I raised dark bruises on their arms and legs, until Bernadette finally moved me to a corner where I could battle bad dreams alone. Even though I then kicked nothing but the walls, she took pity on me. She paid Moses Pillager to make me a special hoop of light split ash, crisscrossed with catgut web, a dreamcatcher. I hung this alongside the crucifix in my corner but it only spun the dreams through, thicker, faster, until I ceased to sleep at all.

I didn't rest until the morning after Mary Pepewas died, alone in my presence, a girl about my age.

When the Pepewas family sent word, Bernadette Morrissey whipped about the house gathering torn cloth for cleaning, her knitting and accounts for the long sickwatch hours. Sophie and Philomena stuck out their tongues and pinched their noses behind their mother's back. Her daughters hated the slops, the smells, the buckets and pans to rinse, so Bernadette let them stay home. She and I walked the road to the place by lantern light, hurrying behind the fat

66

little Pepewas boy sent to fetch us. I was excited to be out in the motionless dark and then Kokoko, the owl, floated off a branch like smoke and called. Bernadette made the sign of the cross and touched me to do the same.

When we arrived, Mary Pepewas had improved, so much so that her family went to sleep one by one, exhausted and trusting in our care. She had the lung sickness, had coughed bright blood, stammered and trembled for hours, but now she sank into a quiet, regular sleep. Bernadette sent me to the barn with the children. I curled in the loft, waiting sleepless and alert until Bernadette handed over the lantern and took my place. It must have been at least halfway to morning. I went into the house and sat on the wood bench beside Mary's bed and watched her as I had never watched anyone before. She had once been homely and fat. Now she was wasted and thin. We had attended school together at the Mission before I traveled down to Argus. I tried to remember something Mary had done or said, some detail. But the only thing I could think of were her thick legs and the torn leather shoes flapping off her feet as she ran from end to end of the dirt yard. I imagined those feet, saw them travel faster until they blurred. I began to doze in waking, and in waking to dream with clear sight. That is when I saw Mary Pepewas begin to change.

She did not stir. She did not arch from the bed or twist to evade death or push it away from her face as it descended, entered, I don't know how. She let it fill her like dark water and then, a narrow-bottomed boat tied to shore, she began to pull away. But she was moored by her jaw, caught, for as the current drew her off her mouth opened, wider, wide as can be, as if she wanted to swallow herself. The waves came and then, soundless, she closed her eyes, strained and tossed. Perhaps, hand over hand, I could have drawn her back to shore, but I saw very clearly that she wanted to be gone. I understood this. That is why I put my fingers in the air between us, and I cut where the rope was frayed down to string.

She drifted. Her face loosened and her mouth shut. I stood when she was gone and called the others into the room, surprised at how light I felt, as though I'd been cut free as well. I hooked my hands on a chair, just to hold steady. If I took off my shoes I would rise into the air. If I took my hands away from my face I would smile. A cool blackness lifted me, out the room and through the door. I leapt, spun, landed along the edge of the clearing. My body rippled. I tore leaves off a branch and stuffed them into my mouth to smother laughter. The wind shook in the trees. The sky hardened to light. And that is when, twirling dizzily, my wings raked the air, and I rose in three powerful beats and saw what lay below.

They were stupid and small, milling behind the lanterned windows. Even Bernadette, who would teach me what I needed to know, appeared simply tired, as though this were no joy. I alone, watching, filled with breath, knew death as a form of grace.

They say, or Bernadette does, that when they found me in the tree later that morning, everyone was shot with fear at the way I hung, precarious, above the ground. They were amazed I could climb there, as the trunk was smooth for seven feet and there were no hand- or footholds of any sort. But I remembered everything, and wasn't in the least surprised. I knew that after I circled, studied, saw all, I touched down on my favorite branch and tucked my head beneath the shelter of my wing. Then I slept, black and dreamless, beautifully complete, as I had not slept since the lockers, as I would now sleep every night.

After that, although I kept the knowledge close, I knew I was different. I had the merciful scavenger's heart. I became devious and holy, dangerously meek and mild. I wore the nuns' castoffs, followed in Bernadette's tracks, entered each house where death was about to come, and then made death welcome. And because I was no widow, as are women who handle the dead, like Bernadette, I toiled the harder. I scrubbed and waxed far into the night, polished whatever poor nickel plate trimmed their stoves, chopped wood, kneaded and then baked the bread that the living would put into their mouths. I learned, from Bernadette, the way to arrange the body, the washing and combing and stopping of its passages, the careful dressing, the final weave of a rosary around the knuckles. I handled the dead until the cold feel of their skin was a comfort, until I no longer bothered to bathe once I left the cabin but touched others with the same hands, passed death on.

We set them praying into the ground if they were Christians, or if unconverted, along the death road of the Old Ones, with an extra pair of shoes. It was no matter to me what happened after life. I didn't care. I accompanied Bernadette, waited for the moment that brought me peace.

In the spring of that year, Misshepeshu went under and wasn't seen much in the waves of the lake anymore. He

69

cracked no boats to splinters and drowned no more girls, but watched us, eyes hollow and gold.

To our minds, Lulu's eyes blazed bright as his. Yet she had the Kashpaws' unmistakable nose, too wide and squashed on the tip. She was good-looking. She had Fleur's coarse, quick-growing hair. Sheer black. She got teeth early, pointed to them with her fat, alert fingers, seemed proud of their sharpness and number. She always demanded to be held, so she was carried in arms till the second summer of her life.

Margaret, who spent most of her time living in her daughter-in-law's home, did a great deal of the carrying. Margaret had grudged Fleur's refusal to leave Pillager land, and fought when Eli took up residence in Fleur's cabin. The lure of a granddaughter was too much, however, and now she and Nector stayed at Matchimanito for days on end, depended on Nanapush to bring them news of what went on in town. They formed a kind of clan, the new made up of bits of the old, some religious in the old way and some in the new. Along with any of the household she could drag, Margaret came to Mass. She tied Lulu against her chest in an old shawl and made the child sit through Benediction, right up front where incense smoke would touch her skin, as though she needed purifying.

Which she did. Lulu was spoiled proud, never humble. She laughed at Father Damien in his skirts, at the nuns in their starched and cutting wimples. She looked eagerly, with quick attention, into the faces of our elders and shrieked at the ridiculous eyes they made. She laughed at everything. The sight of her own feet. My face.

But of course I had got no prettier since Argus.

In fact, I got my growth too fast, stretched long as a hayrake and acquired no softening grace in my features. My forehead wrinkled because I shut my eyes hard against certain sights. My jaw grew and my mouth sank into it. My nose was long. God had overlooked me in the making, given no marks of His favors. I was angles and sharp edges, a girl of bent tin.

Spring was overtaken by the days of dry and fragrant heat. Although I never went empty-handed to Matchimanito Lake and always carried a choice bit of news for Margaret, it was around that time that I began to believe the Kashpaws and Pillagers didn't like to have me around. Not that they ever said as much. When Fleur wasn't busy with other things she claimed she had to do, we played cards late into the night, four of us around the table, me, Fleur, Eli, and Margaret or Nanapush, all with cups of strong coffee at our elbows, and the child asleep, slung in a blanket that was lapped and sewed over two ropes. The ropes hung down, looped, so that whenever Lulu stirred her mother rocked her by swinging her foot beneath the table.

But always, there was something in the air. They held back from me. Margaret ceased to greet me at the door, offered scraps and only baked a fresh loaf when I'd stayed for an hour or two. I felt the chill even more when Fleur and Eli began to keep their distance from each other in my presence, as though I'd gone and told some lie, some tale about the way they acted together.

Yet what was between them was more obvious to me than if they touched. I could not pass between the two of them—the air was busy, filled with sparks and glowing needles, simmering. Their bodies, like ore and lodestones, drew together and repelled me, or, if I stubbornly resisted, loomed close enough to crush. I have heard from others that Margaret reported I got shifty, never met their eyes. But in truth I could only look upon them part by part, never wholly, for it seemed that in relation to each other they swelled and shrank. His hands grew large, covering the deck of cards, his forearms thickened while her waist pinched and her breasts became taut and heavy with response. Some days I saw the signs, the small dents of her teeth on his arm, the scorched moons of bruises on his throat. Or I sensed touching, an odor, a warmth like sun streaming down on skin for an afternoon. In the morning, before they washed in Matchimanito, they smelled like animals, wild and heady, and sometimes in the dusk their fingers left tracks like snails, glistening and wet. They made my head hurt. A heaviness spread between my legs and ached. The tips of my breasts chafed and wore themselves to points and a yawning eagerness gripped me.

I thought I must get married, must find myself a husband. I thought that the reason I was not wanted was just that I was alone. So I cast around the village. I was obvious. Nanapush, who observed too close and teased me with such greed, noticed me at the trading store one day and pointed me out to Napoleon, who said something knowing in reply, some joke, and then set his hand on the back of my neck, indifferent, like I was stock on his farm. I shook free, but saw him in a new way after that. Instead of the grizzled hairs and hard-set mouth, I noticed his strong hips, the width of his neck.

He had a trimmed French mustache and flat dark lips. He had more hair, as it turned out, on his chest, which frightened me at first. There was an old house in the woods, abandoned now and caving in, that had once belonged to a woman and her two weak-brained daughters. He told me to meet him there one day, and I did. It was a hot close afternoon. We didn't speak. I lay down on the floor and, piece by piece, he took off all I wore.

"You're thin as a crane," he said, the only words.

I was awkward too. I twined myself along his full length, but came out longer at the head and feet. The light through the uncaulked boards streamed too harsh and brilliant. With my clothes gone, I saw all the bones pushing at my flesh. I tried to shut my eyes, but couldn't keep them closed, feeling that if I did not hold his gaze he could look at me any way he wanted. So we pressed together with our eyes open, staring like adversaries, but we did not go through with it after all. He stopped for some reason, nothing we said or did, but like a dog sensing the presence of a tasteless poison in its food. We lay quietly. Nothing moved but the mice behind the walls, skittering across the whole afternoon and then through the smothering night, in which I stayed long after he left and imagined a different scene between the two of us.

In my picture, we coupled in a blinding darkness, moved too fast to think. We howled like cats in a manger, dove and bucked like horses in their heat. I snapped him in my beak like a wicket-boned mouse. He crushed me to a powder and spread me across the floor. Yet when morning invaded the empty windows and doors, we woke whole, unhurt, prepared for more pleasure. Our bruised mouths moved on each other and our hands to what they knew. And already, through the bush and down the road, over the next hill, as if the mice had gone running down with gossip, people talked.

But what the people said in fact was far different from what I had them say in fantasy. They laughed. Napoleon took his string of horses and went south, where he would sell them to the teachers down at Sioux. I heard this from Clarence, one night when Bernadette was out stripping clothes from the line. He didn't face me, just talked to the plate with his mouth full.

It cut the half minute that his words hung in the air. Then I said in a cold voice, "He'll be back."

Clarence turned then, and made a mocking face. He was a young man but he had a sense for scandal, a way with numbers like his mother, a big fresh face with regular features and a red bow mouth. Clarence was the one I should have tried for, I saw that, but I also knew what he saw— the pole-thin young woman others did, the hair pulled back and woven into a single braid, the small and staring eyes that did not blink. I could have told him that I had a secret way of drawing Napoleon to me. Or that I knew Napoleon would only travel as far south as I reeled out the tether on which I had him, that when he reached the choking end and jerked back he'd come home. I could have said these things, but I was not even sure I cared. I hadn't liked the weight of Napoleon's hands, their hardened palms. I hadn't liked seeing myself naked, plucked and skinned. I had already satisfied my yearning curiosity. Now I knew that men and women ground their bodies together, sweat and cried out, wept, shoved their hips in motion and fell quiet. Then they lay there and looked at the wall, listening as the mice scratched insistently behind the boards.

The months passed and collected until a year was spent, and I continued to assist Bernadette. Sometimes now I even went out on my own, and when I arrived not even the old ones remembered that I was a virgin and had no dead husband. I came before the priests, appeared in my black clothes, and now when people saw me walking down the road, they wondered who was being taken, man, woman, or child. I was a midwife that they hailed down with both interest and dread. I was their own fate. Somewhere now, in the back of their minds, they knew that these bodies they tended and preened, got drunk, pleasured and refused, fed as often as they could and relieved, these bodies to which they were devoted, all in good time came to me. Yet to some, I was more invisible than ever in my black clothes, and now the picture of my life stared plain enough. Death would pass me over just as men did, and I would live a long, strict life.

I especially missed what Napoleon had begun to show me when I visited the Pillager place. Yet I did not stay away. I went there hoping that Eli would be with Fleur. Now that I understood the way things happened with a man and woman, now that I knew it would not happen to me, I tried to warm my hands at the fire between them.

Jealousy was such a small step to take from that.

One day, although we'd thrown the door open and pushed free the newly bought oiled paper windows, the cabin was still oppressive with late summer heat. We dragged out the table for sitting and played a few hands of pinochle in the beaten dirt yard. Margaret had a ruffed bitch just whelped and slung beneath with blind and dragging pups, whose one intelligence was how to hang on by sucking. The girl, Lulu, played with peas and acorns by the door. Eli came into the yard, slapped three fish on a plank, slit and cleaned them and tossed the entrails down to the snapping dogs.

Fleur was frowning, musing, beating me at some game again. She threw down the cards.

"No challenge," she said. The language rippled from her mouth. "The sloughpumper's got her mind elsewhere."

Fleur underestimated me, thought so little about me it was almost like being despised. Since that night she had carried me to bed in her arms, laid me among the ledgers and balls of twine, I had been no more to her than a piece of wall. Any of her attention that spilled past Eli, she had turned on her child. She taught Lulu too many words, too fast, so that the girl kept up a constant and annoying string of song and talk which the others laughed at and indulged. And the way they dressed her! Even now, although she was playing in the dirt, Lulu wore tiny red bead bracelets and doeskin moccasins, quilled with flower designs. Her bright green dress was cinched around her stomach with a leather belt, and her shining hair was braided tightly. When Fleur lifted her, Lulu gripped her mother's hips with her knees, clung fast. She pinched a blouse button in her fingers and let Fleur rock her. I turned away. I could feel the distance rush between us like cold water from a broken dam, and at the same time I was drawn by Eli's heat, by the warmth of him as he didn't mind anything but his small task. He laid the fish in a pan of water, wiped his hands on the grass, and stirred up a cooking fire in the yard.

I went to help him. At first he was just the man she always had around, some cousin of mine. Then it was like a curtain of water dropped away. I saw the pliable strength of his hips, then his waist, the wiry chest and arms and hollowed throat, the black tail that swung. I saw his thick eyebrows, flat strong nose, turned lips. His youth.

76

From the way he moved, I knew how it would be in his arms. He addressed each task. Absorbed himself in it. He would concentrate that way on me. And I thought, then, when he lifted his eyes and saw me looking, that he knew. For he paused a beat too long.

And it was there, while Fleur and Lulu were inside the house fetching flour, that I put out my hand and let it glide against him. My knuckles grazed an inch of his skin. Then he caught my palm in his. For a moment I thought, with wild certainty, that he would hold my fingers to his lips. But he looked at my hand with curiosity, no intent, and then, like a fish too small to keep, he threw it back.

So I both turned from him and desired him, in hate.

I slept in the big bed with Bernadette's girls again, because after Mary Pepewas's death I never woke, kicked, or bruised them. But then, one night, I dreamed. Eli was near, breathing, hoarse with need yet holding himself away. His hair swung loose and brushed my pillow when he lowered his face. I arched to meet him, swung wide, but never grasped him, not quite. I woke and next to me the girls were sleeping—Philomena, just ten, and Sophie who at fourteen was younger than me. Sophie nested close. Her hair spilled across the pillow and clung between my lips. I lay awake for a long while that night, watching her sleep. She was a pretty girl, with brown hair and eyes, a soft red mouth and a brand new body that did not fatten and teeth that did not rot no matter how many bags of sweets she ate, in secret, beneath the covers of our bed at night.

I began to observe Sophie during the day as well.

The trading store DuCharme gave her candy each time we went to town. Sophie thrust the striped sack in her skirt, doled out the sourballs and gum bite by precious bite. Her legs were fine and long as a filly's, her body already that of a woman. Her lips were almost too full and too red, but still, she was more beautiful than anyone else had noticed, except DuCharme. Waking choked and hot from Eli, another night later on, I listened to her jaws crush the striped shells of peppermints, heard her suck the foam centers, smelled the wild sassafras and licorice she exhaled. The sweetness of her breath was penetrating and her limbs, brushing mine, shifted with absent pleasure at the taste in her mouth. I was older, drank my coffee bitter, cut her hair and toenails, for she was lazy. I was the pretend aunt, and much too serious for penny candy. But as I envisioned her slim brown body, next to me, stretched out in the cotton sheath I'd sewed, it came to me what I would do.

With the dim light cloaking us together, I could almost feel what it was like to be inside Sophie's form, not hunched in mine, not blending into the walls, but careless and fledgling, throwing the starved glances of men off like the surface of a pond, reflecting sky so you could never see the shallow bottom. It was because of that, thinking of the pond and of the men, that I went to the trader a few days later and bought the blue material. I paid for the length with coins that had shut a dead woman's eyes. I stitched the dress right on the girl. She slouched, her hair a tangle, dirt blotching her thighs and elbows, a smell coming off her like duck feathers, oiled and sly. Her bare feet scuffed at the boards, but her eyes showed interest. She was pleased at the color of the flowered calico, at the pull of it across her chest and hips because I sewed it so close there you could see her nipples when they tightened.

Bernadette might have noticed my sudden attentions to

her daughter, except she was busy managing the farm and governing Napoleon. He had returned, and she was suspicious. On a cool morning noisy with the cries of birds, she rounded the corner of the barn and found him caging me with his arms. With her standing there, I pushed him away. I saw the look of surprise, then confirmation, in her eyes and knew no words of mine could avert her conclusion. So I changed the subject, turned the direction of her mind. I suggested that we hire another man to help during hay season. I gave reasons, and I mentioned Eli Kashpaw. She was a practical woman and acknowledged the wisdom. I told her that I would be the one to fetch him.

The next day was fresh, the leaves curled dry around the edges and a faint cold hung in the shadows before the heat lowered. Fleur was sitting on a rock by the lake, shaded by her elegant black umbrella. She twirled it back and forth dreamily. Her skirt was spread like a trap for fish. Lulu stumbled along the shore, chose rocks and threw them at the waves. No mother but Fleur would dare take her daughter to this lake of the monster.

"Eli's in the woods," Fleur said, abrupt, as I approached.

So then I knew she saw more than I thought, and I treaded with care.

"They've got day labor over at the Morrisseys'," I said. "Hay's in the field."

Fleur took a bit of jerky from her pocket and put her teeth to it.

"That's where you're staying." Her voice arched with sarcasm.

He must have told her. They must have had a laugh about my straying hands.

"I'll keep a lookout for him," I said. "Sometimes those Morrisseys pinch a penny when they settle accounts. You have to watch them close."

Fleur's face sharpened as she saw there was more about me than she wanted to know.

"I'll tell him," she finally decided. Her face was all blades.

She was testing, she was thinking, she was going to amuse herself. I knew she'd tell him. And I was right, for not more than two days passed before he arrived at the Morrissey house. By then, I'd traded candles and ribbons for the thing I needed from Moses, who made the dreamcatcher. He gave me the sack of medicine powder, then held my eyes with his and made me tell him whom I meant to snare. He dragged Eli's name from me in a whisper, which caused him great amusement, and then his face twisted. I ran before he howled, and thought of Fleur. Surely this strange cousin of hers would pass my plans on, but already it was too late. I couldn't stop myself. The dust Moses had concocted was crushed fine of certain roots, crane's bill, something else, and slivers of Sophie's fingernails. I would bake it all in Eli's lunch.

From the first day, I knew what I planned was possible. I was there late in the afternoon when Eli walked off the fields into the yard. I waited on the anvil in the shadow of the house, and Sophie was out front, drinking from the windmill trough. She leaned over the water, sucking it like a heifer. The calico clung down her back where she sweat. Her waist was neat and her neck, burnt red where I'd pinned up her hair, was slender as a reed. Eli watched her. When she turned, wiped her mouth on the back of her arm, shook her hands dry, he came forward. He asked if he could have a drink. Then Sophie took the tin cup off its wire hook and held it under the trickle that gushed hard when the wind moved but nearly stopped on days like that one—hot, still, the air heavy with light.

Sophie watched as he took a careful sip, eyes steady over the cup rim; then he tipped all the rest of the water down his chest and asked if he could wash. Sophie nodded and stepped away. Eli swept the drowned moths and grasshoppers to the side and plunged his head quickly in and out. He pushed the water across his cheekbones and down his neck, mopped his face with a handkerchief. He gave Sophie a slow look that she turned from, her face blurred and glowing. She watched her own fingers pick apart a weed, then she threw it down suddenly and ran, kicking up her bare and dirty heels.

Eli stared after her and saw through me, still as the iron wedge I sat on, dark in a cool place. He could not see into the shadow. His eyes never even flickered. I rose after he left, and followed Sophie through the door. I filled her head with ideas, told her how Eli looked at her, what I saw. It was almost too simple, that part, it took no thought or work. She was brainless as a newborn calf.

Yet Sophie had natural ability I came nowhere near. In the late mornings of those next days, she thought to bring him water flavored with ginger, or lemonade that she made with sugar and citric acid. She lingered, tickling her arms with grass stalks, singing, until Clarence sent her back to the house. Each day I made Eli's bannock with a tiny pinch of the charm dust. That was to lay the seeds of wanting. Then, under my encouragement, Sophie put the rest of the food together with her own hands, the bread cut too thick, the meat tough and greasy, the sweet cake flattened by her clumsy knife. She saved her candy for him, offered cinnamon sticks fuzzy with lint, sweets she carried in her shirt or pocket. He took them. Her supply dwindled. Napoleon teased her about the way Eli's eyes lingered, and Clarence vowed to kill him if he laid a hand where he shouldn't. I was satisfied. Nights, I heard Sophie's jaws crack the last few peppermints to pieces, heard her determined chewing. She was ready when the day came.

There were just the three of us, Sophie and Eli and me, on the farm. Bernadette had taken the youngest into town, and Clarence and Napoleon were helping a cousin repair some harvest tool while Eli pitched a last load of hay. I made Sophie assist with baking. Mounds of dough, sweetened and sour, filled our dishpans. Into the first, the one for Eli, I kneaded the last of the potion. We let the loaves rise under towels, punched them down. Sophie gazed out the door, scratched her flank, grudgingly used the comb I put into her hand.

"There he is," she pointed. But I didn't look. I slid his twice-risen bread into the oven. I could see him in my mind's eye, his worn blue shirt and sash, his workpants rubbed smooth across his knees and back end, his gleaming swatch of hair, the labored pitch and swing of a man far off, stacking hay. It took the baking time of one batch for him to work his way over to the slough, the deep one that stayed fresh all year. He halted where it was cool. I tipped the baked bread from the pan. The crust was barely hardened before Sophie filled the water jug, took a block of butter, tucked the loaf into the crook of her arm and slammed out the door.

I went out too. I slipped into the woods and took the

hidden path around the edge of the field, the path that led straight to the slough. I concealed myself at an opening in the brush, looked out and saw the two of them on the ground beside the haypile that Eli was making, a new one, next to the old stack cows had eaten around the bottom until it looked like a giant mushroom. Eli sat with his legs crossed before him. The bread was in his mouth. Her hand was on the earth between them. I saw Sophie pick a stalk of beard-grass and run it up his arm. He smiled at her, spread butter on the rest of the loaf with his hunting knife, chewed. He drank from the jug, swatted a fly from the air, and leaned back on his elbows. And then, as I crouched in the cove of leaves, I turned my thoughts on the girl and entered her and made her do what she could never have dreamed of herself. I stood her in the broken straws and she stepped over Eli, one leg on either side of his chest. Standing there, she slowly hiked her skirt.

She was naked underneath, as always, when it was hot. She bent, then pressed her bare self to his chest. He passed his tongue over his lips, shook his head as if to clear it. A thin panic shot through me. I thought Moses had failed. But then Sophie took a last bit of soft gum-red licorice from her mouth and pressed it between his lips. He moved his hands up her thighs, beneath the tucked billow of her skirt. She shivered and I dug my fingers through the tough claws of sumac, through the wood-sod, clutched bark, shrank backward into her pleasure.

He lifted her and brought her to the water. She stood rooted, dazed, not alert enough to strip off her dress. He went in, shucked off his clothing and threw it on the bank. She waited in shallow mud, then waded in, obedient. They fell on each other. He ran his mouth over her face, bit her shoulder through the cloth, held her head back by the pale brown strands and licked her throat. He pulled her hips against him, her skirt floating like a flower. Sophie shuddered, her eyes rolled to the whites. She screamed God's name and blood showed at her lip. Then she laughed.

And I, lost in wild brush, also laughed as they began to rock and move. They went on and they went on. They were not allowed to stop. They could drown, still moving, breathe water in exhaustion. I drove Eli to the peak and then took his relief away and made him start again. I don't know how long, how many hours. Their bodies would grow together and their skins hang loose. Their breasts and thighs would wrinkle like a toad's, their faces puff, their eyes bloat, yet they would move and move. I was pitiless. They were mechanical things, toys, dolls wound past their limits.

I let them stop eventually, I don't know how or when. The sun was lower and on the hill appeared the tiny shadows of the men. As if cut from puppet strings, Eli lunged to the bank and clutched his trousers to his stomach, worked his way through the reeds and staggered past me, so close I could have touched him, and on into the darker trees.

Alone now, Sophie floundered to the side, found her balance and then stood, drenched, a child. She peered into the cattails that had closed behind him and called out. I answered.

"You'll have a switching," I cried. "Get on up to the house!"

But she sank to her knees in the sour mud, hung her mouth open and went limp so that I had to drag her, stubborn and bewildered, across the fields.

. . .

I scalded the water for the girl's bath that night, and added it to cold. I peeled off her clothes, showed Bernadette where she had bled, where the dress ripped. I told her my suspicions—I pretended to guess—but it was Sophie herself who convinced Bernadette my words were true. The girl brooded, more composed than she'd ever been, her lips hot and thick from kissing, but clamped shut. Her gaze was trained on the floor and she refused to meet our eyes or to speak. Clarence had loaded his gun and now he argued with Bernadette about whether or not to pay a visit to Eli. He could not decide whether anything had happened. Only the aunt, Pauline Kashpaw, knew the truth and perched on it.

I stayed in my chair and cleaned ripe gooseberries until my fingers and then my hands grew dark and stained. Until Sophie walked quietly to bed, until Clarence stopped bickering, put the gun away and slept. I remained in my place, let the lantern burn low, and continued to pinch the beaks from the berries the Bijius had sold us.

It mattered very little what these Morrisseys thought or decided. I knew what I'd done. And as the night continued, fear forced itself into my mind. I had gone too far. The last part, where I had not let them stop, where I had tested my influence, must have surely given it away. Eli would know, but that was safe. It was not like the time he threw back my hand. He could not laugh to Fleur without betraying his own crime. It was Sophie I worried about, so still now, something forming in her face like thought.

I mulled the situation over till the lamp burned out, and still I didn't move. In the dark, I finally thought what I could do. I must have slept sometime after I'd found my answer because, when the light went gray and the sun broke through the trees, I started awake in the chair and the berries spilled about my feet.

Later on that day, I got Bernadette alone. We were hanging clothes along wires strung between three little scrub oaks.

"I did see them," I said to her. "It was more than a suspicion, but I didn't want to tell."

"Sit down," she said, her face grave and stern. She swiveled to make sure no one would hear what we said as we settled on rocks between the drying shirts.

"I followed her because I was afraid of what would happen, but I was too late. She made the first move." I averted my face, as if in shame. "I hid. I called from the woods. That's when Eli broke away from her and ran."

"So," said Bernadette. Her face went grimmer. She rose and walked into the house. I heard her laying into Sophie with a strap, and I felt it, too, the way I'd absorbed the pleasure at the slough, the way I felt everything that happened to Fleur. I ran in behind Bernadette and when she cocked her arm back, about to strike Sophie's back, already welted and burned, I caught her by the elbow and said, "God's mercy!" The strap dropped. Bernadette stumbled to her daughter and began to weep, but the girl was not affected. She seemed to have acquired something new in her sleep. Intelligence is the closest thing that it resembled, for she looked at me, her brown eyes clear across her mother's shoulder.

"It's you should ask for mercy," she said, "death's bony whore."

Which excited Bernadette past weeping, into a state of

anguish over Sophie where she choked on her own spittle, screamed piercingly, grabbed at motes in the air. I had to calm her, saying she hadn't heard right, that she should sip hot milk. But she would not be tamed and lit, that very hour, on exactly the solution for which I'd hoped. She decided to send Sophie far away, to Grand Forks where a strict aunt lived, devout and childless, next door to a church.

Bernadette wrote a letter the very next day, and walked into town to put it in the Agent's hand. She returned with an empty trunk of flowered cardboard, balanced on one shoulder. This was for Sophie's clothing—the two gowns I washed, dried, and ironed, the hair ribbon and the good shoes, the other dress besides the blue calico, a comb and her peg doll. All of this was laid in the trunk while Sophie watched, vacant and stubborn, as though this had nothing to do with her. Even on the day she left, the weather cold and deepening, she didn't say goodbye or notice us at all when Napoleon hoisted her onto the front seat of the wagon, nor did she seem to care whether the flowered trunk accompanied her, braced carefully within the load of wood that Napoleon would trade. She shrugged off the blanket I draped around her shoulders, and looked straight ahead when the cart lurched onto the road.

She looked so stiff and dazed that we never would have predicted how, ten minutes from the house, she fooled us by jumping off the cart.

Sophie landed on reservation ground, but nowhere near the turnoff to Matchimanito. How could we know she would run straight across bush to the Pillagers'? I say she fooled us, but not on purpose, for it was Fleur's purpose that the girl plunged toward, through raspberry pickers and knots

87

of leaves, unaware of pain and helpless, drawn there against herself.

Napoleon was so disgusted that he did not come home but simply went to town and sold the wood for drink. So I had no notion of Sophie's flight until the next day, when I left early and walked the five miles to Matchimanito. Right away, stepping into the clearing around Fleur's cabin, I saw Sophie.

She was kneeling in the yard, stiff as a soldier, hands a steeple, wearing the blue calico dress. She stared at Fleur's door and did not blink. I neared her cautiously, waved my hands at her face, called her name, but she stayed mute. I bent to her side and, desperately, I poked her.

"No need for that," said Fleur. Her approach had been soundless. She smiled at me steady and hungry, teeth glinting, and I saw again the wolf those men met down in Argus, the one who laughed and stuffed their money in her dress.

I bolstered myself, however, by not taking entire responsibility for what had happened.

It was true that Sophie was innocent. And yet it was also true that the devil found an empty vessel, lazy, crammed with greed for little pleasures.

"Eli's been on the trapline," said Fleur. She pondered my face for a long moment. "But the fur's no good till late fall."

Her strong throat was bare. She wore a red blouse and a long full black skirt, and had her hair wound around the back of her head, coiled tightly.

I looked her in the eye. The weight of my danger gave me courage.

"Eli was running through the woods with his pants in his arms, last time I saw him." I nicked my chin out. "Away from her."

The smile on Fleur's face went so broad and dazzling I had to blink, even though I don't believe what the old men say. I don't believe the Pillagers could harm that easily.

"He's hiding from you like a dog," I cried. The grain of truth in all I said kept my voice from pitching.

I pointed to Sophie, who still hadn't moved, who knelt rigid. My mouth opened but my speech failed. The door to the cabin swung and Margaret emerged with a bowl, bread, a spoon. She stooped and tried to force a bit of meat broth into Sophie's mouth. But the girl clamped her jaws and did not alter her expression.

"Put it down," said Fleur.

Margaret left the bowl and we went into the house. Fleur paced and twig by twig made a show of constructing a fire for cooking. Margaret worked silently on a beaded tobacco bag until the light began to dim. Sometime after the lamp was lit, we heard, or rather sensed, Sophie topple.

"Let's take her inside," Margaret proposed.

But Fleur said, "Throw a blanket on her." So I went out and wrapped a blanket around Sophie's huddled form, and then we all went to bed. But I was afflicted with the old lack of sleep. I tossed in my covers, on the floor near the stove, working my mind back and forth on the problem like a saw, until at last I had it all in pieces, and understood that I couldn't put it back together.

The next morning Sophie was on her knees again, her head thrown back, arms stiff at her sides and fists clenched. Her hair blew in a circle around her head in the windy dawn. The bowl of soup had tipped, its contents disappeared, consumed by her or by the dogs. She didn't move, minutes later, when the drenching rain poured. Margaret stamped out yet again, grumbling complaints. She yelled for Fleur, but there was no answer. Then she called for me. I would have gone to help except that Fleur's look stopped me. The old woman chopped four poles with her hatchet and pounded them into the soft earth around the girl. She draped an oilskin over this, made a rude little sagging shelter with Sophie beneath it, wet and wretched and still.

"Heartless!" cried Margaret angrily, coming in the door. I looked away. But Fleur said to her, "I have my reasons, as you'll see."

The day wore on, and Sophie didn't move, not even when Eli walked into the yard with six ducks on a string.

I was looking out the door when this happened. He didn't pay me any attention whatsoever, of course, just stopped in front of Sophie. He stood for some time. Then he pumped himself full of false bravery. It was visible, the way he did this. Cocking his hip, counting the handsome ducks, pressing a fist to his forehead once, shaking himself taller and straighter, he walked in the door.

Perhaps I had watched something change in him, right there, from boy to man, from man to deceiver of women. For he was calm when he entered, puzzled as anyone would have a right to be. He went immediately to Fleur, guiltless, confused.

I watched closely, saw the workings clearly for a moment, as I had the time Dutch James pried off the back of his watch.

The expression on Fleur's face was open lines. Then she saw. The lines shaded in, the pattern darkened. She rose and turned from Eli. She walked to the stove, grabbed a fork to tend a pan of sizzling venison. She said nothing, but when he stepped near and laid his hand upon her arm she simply moved her arm away. That's when he knew. He turned and retreated, left the door hanging open behind. We didn't hear which way he went through the woods.

Fleur seemed to have no use for me after that, and I escaped. The road that met the main turnoff to the Pillagers' was beaten smooth, easier to follow now, and as I crossed it the cold cut like knives. I went like someone in a dream, exhausted and anxious. It was one of those harbinger evenings, freezing and clouded, a night of first frost. The air smelled wet and dry at once, like snow. I got back to the Morrisseys' and the two men were eating a late supper that they'd cooked for themselves—fried meat, bread and onions.

"Where the hell you been?" Napoleon asked. His talk was still rough with drink, and he smelled of the barn, where he'd slept most likely.

"The Pillagers'."

"Blanket Indians," he said in an ugly voice. "I don't want you going out there."

I put fire in the stove to heat some oatmeal for my supper. Clarence slipped out the door, and suddenly Napoleon was at my shoulder. He reached into the waist of my blouse and spread his hand across the wing of my back.

"They've got Sophie out there," I said, and after a moment he moved away. I heard the door open and then slam, heard the pound of his boots and Clarence's fade down the road. I boiled a pan of milk, ate standing. Then I wrapped myself in one of Bernadette's winter shawls and went out, after them, back along the trail to Matchimanito.

What happened after that is commonly known, part of our history. The men arrived. They saw Sophie, still kneeling, tried to pick her up and found she would not budge. They put their weight to her, tried at least to tip her so they could drag her, but they could not shift her one small inch and finally backed away, their fear and confusion gathering. They bolted down the path, passed me without a word.

There was no change in Sophie when I got there, and I did not leave her side. Her skin was cold to my touch, waxy with death and gritty with soot from the embers of the little fire Margaret Kashpaw had built. The snow began to fall, cloaking us together. I stirred the fire, brought wood. I pulled the shawl around the two of us.

Napoleon and Clarence had run for the priest, knocked on his door in the dark of night. He was roused by their terror and excitement, and followed them into the nave of the church, where Sister Anne kept a late vigil before the treasure of the mission, our Blessed Virgin.

In the years to come, I learned Her in each detail.

She was perfect, made of finest French plaster, dressed in the midday sky, a sequined satin robe and pleated veil. She was cast in the act of stepping past the moon at its limit. Stars turned at Her feet, which rested full weight on a lively serpent. The snake was bent to strike and colored a poison green. The Virgin's foot was small, white, and marvelously bare. Her blood was so pure that it would overcome the venom in any wound. How well She knew this. She scorned to look down. Her eyes were fixed on the place before Her where sinners knelt, and Her hands were open, offered to their anguish. In one palm a drop of blood was painted. In the other, a yellow sun shone. She had a full figure curving to a slim waist, broad hips. Her throat was strong and milky white, corded with straps of muscle.

Her face was more than simply saintlike or beautiful. The nose was large, with a small bump to the left, and Her lips full, half parted as though to blurt a secret. Her brows were thick and Her eyes were light brown. And, this was strange, they held the same lively curious suspension as the snake's.

Lit by the mystery, Clarence leapt across the thin wood rail and grabbed Her from the church's niche.

Sister Saint Anne, small and passionate, sprang up in response and gave chase, keeping well within range of Clarence through the miles, even in her heavy robes. Napoleon and Father blundered anxiously along the half-lit road. I was still caught in this web, huddled in the Pillager yard near Sophie, when Clarence broke into the clearing with the statue in his arms. A moment later Sister Anne arrived, breathless, her skirts stitched and bunched with cockleburrs and twigs, her delicate face glowing, a blur in the dim light.

She didn't have to speak. The force of her determination was enough.

Clarence stood uncertain, shocked and thrilled by his courage, but now unable to imagine the next step, what to do with the statue, how it could be used to dislodge his sister.

Sister Saint Anne stood firm, ordered him to surrender, and this time Clarence lowered the Virgin so that She gazed down upon the place where I knelt with Sophie. The moon's light spilled over the trees and revealed the blessed face, still and fascinated.

"Hail Mary, full of grace!" began the nun, in gratitude. While she prayed she edged closer to the statue and beat at Clarence with her robe so that he retreated. When the prayer was done, she stood next to the Virgin protectively.

Margaret was in the yard, her gray hair unplaited on her shoulders, a blanket around her. She put the lamp she carried on the ground, and we knelt in the yard of pressed earth as Clarence talked, or tried to. He stumbled. He seemed foolish and stunned as Sister Saint Anne questioned him for sense. "You saw what now? Repeat?" And so, because they were wrapped in explanations, I was first witness to the occurrence, and in fact the only other witness besides Sophie, for I never told what I saw, as I believed it was meant for the girl alone, and for myself, my private miracle upon which no sounding trumpet should intrude.

I have no idea which prayer I spoke that night, I cannot recall the words. I cannot remember my lips moving, whether there were notions in my head. If my knees hurt, if I hungered, if I felt anything—that's lost. I do see uneven light, so small in the vast dark, dim on the two faces that gazed at one another: the Virgin, so curious and alive, and Sophie, dull. The girl's face tipped up, slack, less human than the small statue, who offered Her blooded palm, Her shining sun. The Virgin stared down. Her brow was clear, Her cheeks bone-pale, Her lips urgently forming a secret syllable, all of a sudden trembled. That's when I saw the first tear.

There were more. Although Her expression never changed, She wept a hail of rain from Her wide brown eyes. Her tears froze to hard drops, stuck invisibly in the corners of Her mouth, formed a transparent glaze along Her column throat, rolled down the stiff folds of Her gown and struck the poised snake. It was then that the commotion took place, not over the statue's tears, which no one else noticed, but over Sophie, who tried to rise but could not, as her knees were horribly locked, who fell sprawled in the new snow.

Clarence grabbed her under the arms and hoisted her

against his chest. Napoleon stumbled into the yard and gaped like a child when he saw that the girl was loose. Father entered and looked questions at Sister Anne, but she was silent, a puzzle. He should have observed me. I kept my place, kneeling in the Virgin's sight. Our gazes were locked now, and no one noticed when I put out my hand and scooped the hardened tears that lay scattered at Her feet. They resembled ordinary pebbles of frozen quartz, the kind that children collect and save. I dropped them into my skirt pocket and did not imagine how the warmth of my legs would melt them back to tears again, which happened, on the way home, so that by the time I got to the Morrissey house the only proof was the damp cloth that soon dried, and my memory, which sharpened on the knowledge.

For many months afterward I brooded on what I'd seen. Perhaps, I thought at first, the Virgin shed tears as She looked at Sophie Morrissey, because She herself had never known the curse of men. She had never been touched, never known the shackling heat of flesh. Then later, after Napoleon and I met again and again, after I came to him in ignorance, after I could not resist more than a night without his body, which was hard, pitiless, but so warm slipping out of me that tears always formed in my eyes, I knew that the opposite was true.

The sympathy of Her knowledge had caused Her response. In God's spiritual embrace She experienced a loss more ruthless than we can imagine. She wept, pinned full-weight to the earth, known in the brain and known in the flesh and planted like dirt. She did not want Him, or was thoughtless like Sophie, and young, frightened at the touch of His great hand upon Her mind.

Fall 1917–Spring 1918
Manitou-geezis
Strong Spirit Sun

—

There was nothing to say when Eli showed at my door. His hands were open and lifeless, hung at his sides. The hair flowed thick and loose down one cheek, as if he were in mourning. I saw his gun, tied across the pack on his shoulders, and a small bundle which he handed to me. When I opened the cloth I saw he'd brought me a stash of flour, lard, sugar, and I knew that he wanted to stay. I finally said to him, "You best sit down and have a plate of stew." So he came in, but he wouldn't eat. I suppose he could see for himself that the meat in the pot was only one poor gopher that should have hibernated while it could. He sat on the bed while I ate, but wouldn't look at me, or talk. I got weary of his shuttered face.

"I'm an old man who doesn't have much time left," I hinted.

He took a deep breath, let it out with sad force.

"Ah, the wind has come up!" I encouraged. But now he glared at me, annoyed that his advisor should fail to understand the serious nature of his problem. I understood well enough, however. I took my chair to the window for the fading light and looked at some catalogues and some letters from the land court that had come by mail. A system of post was still a new and different thing to Indians, and I was marked out by the Agent to receive words in envelopes. They were addressed to Mr. Nanapush, and I saved every one I got. I had a skin of them tied and stowed beneath my bed.

Fearing he had lost my interest, Eli mumbled some fierce words to the top of the table and locked his hands together. He knotted and unknotted his fingers until the knuckle-bones made irritating cracks.

"Spread that fire," is all I said, "the wood burns too hot and the sticks are snapping."

He wrung out his fingers, prodded the fire for a while, and fell back in his seat. Next I began to hear the sound of his clenched teeth grinding together, and finally he moaned between his lips.

"How much a man endures!"

"What man?" I said.

"This one!" He sank his face against his palms, and then, most impressive of all, let his head fall with a crash onto my table.

"Lucky my table is made of solid wood too."

"Uncle, have pity on your poor nephew!" he demanded angrily.

"My nephew already has sufficient pity on himself."

"You don't care for me either," he said in a bitter voice, pulling at the long messy flow of his locks. "None of them cares for me anymore."

I knew he was too full of vanity to remove a single hair.

"Some men would pull out a handful or two over what they've done," I told him, bending close. "Look at mine, so thin in spots there's almost nothing. I once shared your weakness—but for women, not little girls."

"She was no little girl!" He came to attention, stirred by the injustice of my judgment. "And besides, I was witched!"

"That's no good, " I counseled, shaking my head. "Fleur has known weak men before, and won't believe that excuse."

"All right," he countered, "but listen to this. *She* has done worse now. And I won't go back to her. She frightens me."

"At last." I continued to turn the dry, sharp pages of my papers. Between this unpromising winter, the pain in my hip that made me feel so poor I could not hunt, and the wholesale purchase of our allotment land by whites, the problems of Eli Kashpaw were of thin consequence, and yet he insisted on pelting me to death with grass.

"Look, fool," I said. "Open your eyes. Even your baby brother has a better grasp of what is going on. We're offered money in the agreements, cash for land. What will you do with the money?"

"Right now?" Eli asked in a belligerent, stalling way.

"Yes," I said, "what would you do with fifty dollars this moment?"

"I'd drink it up," he said in a pouting voice, daring my wrath even though I knew he rarely drank. I gave him no satisfaction, just kept the argument going.

"Like many," I said, "you'd wake with no place to put your foot down."

"I don't want to live around here anyway!" he yelled in rage.

I threw down the papers. "That's all you think about! You!"

Satisfied that he'd raised my temper, pretending he'd got my sympathy, Eli now busied himself with the cold stew. He gulped it all down as if it held tender beef, which we had not seen since the government issue. When he was done he leaned back and, without meaning to, his face registered the flat spoiled taste of the gopher meat. And with that, the first hint of pity for me. But I wanted none.

"I got a herd of this Indian beef corralled out in the woodpile and branded the government way," I told him. "I'm planning on holding a roundup."

He couldn't let himself laugh, so he punished me by staring blankly. He rolled a bit of tobacco and smoked to cut the edge of the grease.

He thought aloud after a while. "If Fleur was only in the church I could go there, get forgiveness by the priest, and then she would have to forget what happened."

He looked over at me, waiting with new hope for some reaction. But I was so disgusted at his foolish reasoning that I'd begun to wonder whether I would even help him. So many other things were on my mind. I had already given Father Damien testimony on this Anishinabe land, which was nibbled at the edges and surrounded by farmers waiting for it to go underneath the gavel of the auctioneer. There were so few of us who even understood the writing on the papers. Some signed their land away with thumbs and crosses.

As a young man, I had made my reputation as a government interpreter, that is, until the Beauchamp Treaty signing, in which I said to Rift-In-A-Cloud, "Don't put your thumb in the ink." One of the officials understood and I lost my job. All of this could not have concerned Eli less. Now he put out the cigarette, grinding it onto the stove and saving the shred of tobacco. He kept looking hopeful, waiting for advice which he did not deserve.

"Lay your blankets down anywhere you want," I said to Eli. There was only the floor of beaten dirt, rock cold in the winter even by the stove. I expected that such constant discomfort would drive him home. He was disappointed, but knelt meekly and covered himself with the rough brown robe.

"My boy," I said into the dark after we were lying without sleep. "They'll eat much worse than gopher out there without a man to hunt. Margaret's no treaty Indian to get her rations in town."

Eli gave a harsh laugh. "Come winter, Fleur will chop a hole in the ice and fish the lake."

"Until then?"

"Until then, she's a good shot."

After six days I could not bear to hear any more from Eli. Each day of snow seemed endless, trapped with a sulking boy. Eli paced, muttered, slept, and also ate my cupboard completely bare, down to the last potato, and emptied the little bundle he brought, too, which would have lasted me the whole evil month. We went two days without anything but grease and crumbs of bread. On the seventh day I handed him his gun. He looked at it in surprise, but finally went north. I went out on my own, checking snares. I had caught some beardgrass, a clump of gray fur, a small carcass picked clean overnight by an owl, and a rabbit that was no good, full of worm. I went home and built the fire, drank some tea of dried nettles and considered that by the end of what looked to be a worse winter than I'd feared, I might be forced to boil my moccasins. That was one good thing at least. I hadn't taken to wearing tradestore boots of dyed leather. Those can kill you. After a while, I went and looked into the floursack, which I knew was already empty, and it was still empty. That's when I lay down.

In my fist I had a lump of charcoal, with which I blackened my face. I placed my otter bag upon my chest, my rattle near. I began to sing slowly, calling on my helpers, until the words came from my mouth but were not mine, until the rattle started, the song sang itself, and there, in the deep bright drifts, I saw the tracks of Eli's snowshoes clearly.

He was wandering, weak from his empty stomach, not thinking how the wind blew or calling on the clouds to cover the sky. He did not know what he hunted, what sign to look for or to follow. He let the snow dazzle him and almost dropped his gun. And then the song picked up and stopped him until he understood, from the deep snow and light hard crust, the high wind and rolling clouds, that everything around him was perfect for killing moose.

He had seen the tracks before, down near a frozen shallow slough. So he went there, knowing a moose is dull and has no imagination, although its hearing is particularly keen. He walked carefully around the rim of the depression. Now he was thinking. His vision had cleared and right away he saw the trail leading over the ice and back into the brush and overgrowth. Immediately, he stepped downwind and branched away, walked parallel and then looped back to find the animal's trail. He tracked like that, never right behind it, always careful of the wind, cautious on the harsh ground, gaining on his webbed shoes as the moose floundered and broke through the crust with every step until finally it came to a stand of young saplings, and fed.

Now the song gathered. I exerted myself. Eli's arms and legs were heavy, and without food he could not think. His mind was empty and I so feared that he would make a mistake. He knew that after the moose fed it would always turn downwind to rest. But the trees grew thicker, small and tightly clumped, and the shadows were a darker blue, lengthening.

Eli's coat, made by Margaret, was an old gray army blanket lined with the fur of rabbits. When he took it off and turned it inside out, so that only the soft pelts would brush the branches and not betray him as he neared, I was encouraged. He took his snowshoes off and left them in a tree. He stuffed his hat into his pocket, made his gun ready and then, pausing and sensitive for movement, for the rough shape, he slowly advanced.

Do not sour the meat, I reminded him now, *a strong heart moves slowly*. If he startled the moose so that adrenaline flowed into its blood, the meat would toughen, reveal the vinegar taste of fear.

Eli advanced with caution. The moose appeared. I held it in my vision just as it was, then, a hulking male, brown and unsuspicious in the late ordinary light of an afternoon. The scrub it stood within was difficult and dense all around, ready to deflect Eli's bullet.

But my song directed it to fly true.

The animal collapsed to its knees. Eli crashed from his hiding place, too soon, but the shot was good and the animal was dead. He used a tree limb to roll it on its back and then with his knife, cut the line down the middle. He was so cold he was almost in tears, and the warmth of the carcass dizzied him. To gain strength for the hard work ahead he carefully removed the liver, sliced off a bit. With a strip of cloth torn from the hem of his shirt, he wrapped that piece, sprinkled it with tobacco, and buried it under a handful of snow. Half of the rest, he ate. The other he saved for me.

He butchered carefully, but fast as possible, according to my instructions. One time in his youth, he had pierced the stomach of a deer with his knife, spreading its acids through the meat, and I'd hardly spoken to him all the rest of that day. He put his jacket right side out again, smeared it with tallow from a packet in his shirt, then quickly cut off warm slabs of meat and bound them to his body with sinew so that they would mold to fit him as they froze. He secured jagged ovals of haunch meat to his thighs, then fitted smaller rectangles down his legs, below the knees. He pressed to himself a new body, red and steaming, swung a roast to his back and knotted its ligaments around his chest. He bound a rack of ribs across his hat, jutting over his face, and tied them on beneath his chin. Last of all, he wrapped new muscles, wide and thick, around each forearm and past his elbows. What he could not pack, he covered with snow and branches, or hoisted laboriously into the boughs of an ash. He was too heavily laden to hide it all and the light was failing, so he fetched his snowshoes, then dragged the hide a distance away from the meat cache and left it for distraction. It was dusk then, and the walk was long.

There is a temptation, when it is terribly cold and the burden is heavy, to quicken pace to warm the blood. The body argues and steps fast, but the knowledge, informed by tales of hunters frozen with the flesh of their own bounty, resists. I know it well. Eli had become a thing of such cold by now, that, if he sweat, the film on his skin would freeze and draw from his blood all life, all warmth.

Without opening my eyes on the world around me, I took the drum from beneath my bed and beat out footsteps for Eli to hear and follow. Each time he speeded I slowed him. I strengthened the rhythm whenever he faltered beneath the weight he bore. In that way, he returned, and when I could hear the echo of his panting breath, I went outside to help him, still in my song.

He glowed, for the meat strapped to him had frozen a marbled blue. The blood from the moose was flour on his coat and on his face. His features were stiff, the strength in his limbs near exhausted. I freed him from the burden he held to his chest, and carried it home in my arms. He followed. I severed the rest from Eli's body and stashed it outside, in the lean-to. The meat stood on its own in pieces, a moose transformed into the mold of Eli, an armor that would fit no other.

He was stockstill, reluctant to move, his mouth dried open as I pulled him through the door. I took off his clothes, found the piece of saved liver under his arm, and ate it. Then I put a drop of water between his lips, wrapped him in a quilt and led him near the stove. I removed the kidneys and heart from Eli's pocket and cut them into smaller sections. My hands shook as I prepared the pieces with salt. My mouth watered as I put them in the fire and at the smell of meat roasting, I almost wept. I gave the first cut to Eli, who fell on it gratefully. As I put my share into my mouth, as I swallowed it, I felt myself grow solid in the chair. Lit by the burning stove, everything around me sharpened. Thoughts returned.

"You're my son," I said, moved by the scorched taste, "you're my relative."

Eli was pleased, nudged a bone into the fire. He was, as you remember, only nineteen around this time. So what he told me, coaxed out by warmth and our fill of meat, by exhaustion and by his great relief in coming back at all, might have been a fresh mind at work, a young man who took in too much, too fast, who overspent his own heart, who could not bear to face his downfall, who imagined, who was lost in the spirit, and both disgusted with his betrayal and desperate for Fleur.

He told me this:

The first time after Sophie, he stayed away from Fleur only long enough to know he couldn't. He returned, and she let him back in the house. But she refused to speak, refused to touch, refused to cook a morsel for him. Being with her and not with her was almost worse than being alone. After three days of Fleur's avoidance, he longed for her with the vigor of their first encounters, when, and I now ask your indulgence for I can only repeat what I remember, even to a granddaughter, those two had coupled outdoors, against trees, down on pine-needle couches or out in the bare yard. After a week, he needed her with twice the force of their first meetings, and after two he was in desperate pain. His blood pounded at the rustle of her skirts. If she brushed him by accident his skin felt scorched. The fire spread. He strained for her like a flame toward air. Nights were even worse. For she suffered him a corner of the bed and from his chill place he could feel her warmth and smell the dark green-smoked weight of her hair.

After he had struggled with his need, he always fell into a long sleep, exhausted from enduring Fleur's indifference. But one night, perhaps because the white moon flooded the yard, he stayed awake, coiled and uncoiled the situation in his mind, tried to see the shape of it. That was when he felt Fleur move. Stealthily, smooth as an otter sliding from a log, she crept off the bed and then, seconds later, was out the door. He heard the latch fall softly back into place, and then he followed her, waking no one. The night was radiant and too cold for bathing, although a movement of branches in the lower corner of the clearing told him Fleur had taken the path that led down to the lake. He went that way too and shrugged through the brush on shore just in time to see Fleur step from her rough sleeping shift and walk, stripped and limber, hair hanging deep black, through a swath of light into the waters of Matchimanito.

The calm ripples closed above her head, and there was nothing to see but the moon glinting off each small disturbance. He held his breath, waiting for Fleur to surface, and then threw himself forward, dived toward the place she had disappeared. Repeatedly, breaking through an ice crust, so shocked his lungs squeezed shut, so horrified he was impervious, he pulled himself further into the water and swept a wide arc with his arms. And then, much later, he didn't quite know how, he slogged back to shore and curled, half frozen and mindless, against a great twisted root.

He was still lying there when Fleur stepped out.

. . .

Eli watched me for some reaction, some older man's wisdom of this event. For a long while I studied the wood, scored and bitten by fire along its chains of growth. I watched the coals flare and fall apart. I added more wood, sent the glare of heat into our faces. I looked at him. There was less of a boy there. I spoke as if I had heard this all before.

"You didn't leave home after that," I said to him. "You waited until now, all these months?"

He nodded. There was more.

"I was stupid, couldn't understand. She went there other nights. Sometimes I woke and her hair was a damp braid tossed against me and once, from along her neck, I picked a curl of black weed from the bottom of the lake."

"She liked to bathe," I countered. "She's got a good set of lungs."

Eli regarded me with hard eyes, with doubt of my understanding, and I saw he had convinced himself the other way.

"The lake is frozen black. The snow is deep, to my chest. The last time Fleur and I had relations was before I went to work for the Morrisseys, during harvest."

He kept his eyes steadily upon me in a rude way, so then I guessed.

"You think that your wife is pregnant."

"Maybe. Not by me." Eli leaned back into the shadows, folded his arms tight against himself in righteous satisfaction.

"You're a fool."

"Don't tell me that, old man. You weren't there."

"You're right," I said, "little boy. I never felt the water,

107

how cold it was. I never felt how warm it was either, last August in the slough."

We were tense in silence. Then I couldn't contain my words. "I helped you with this woman you couldn't handle, who scares off sensible men. I taught you how to get her on your own without medicine. I gave you certain items by which I remembered my last wife. I took you in. And before long, you're so bored you cannot resist a Morrissey, and so stupid you imagine your wife is pregnant when she's not."

"She could be," he flared. "I dreamed how it will look, strange and fearful, bulging eyes, maybe with a split black tail."

I couldn't help myself. I laughed.

"You're a pair," I said. "You and your mother. Inventive."

He shut his mouth.

"Well I've got an opinion," I said after a time, "since you asked. It's a good sign that your wife works to make you jealous. Worse if she didn't. She wants to keep both you and her pride." Eli made to protest, but I gave him no opportunity. "And now, if you listen instead of complain," I said, "I'm going to take pity on that poor lonely mistake you keep hid in your pants and tell you how to get Fleur back."

He flushed, and I continued.

"It's like this. You've got to start all over. The first time you pursued Fleur you had to make her think you were a knowledgeable, capable man, but now it is the opposite. She has to pity you as I do, only more. You have to cut yourself down in her eyes until you're nothing, a dog, so low it won't matter if she lets you crawl back."

He looked ill, suspicious, argumentative, but then the

trials of the day overcame him and he finally gave up. I banked the fire in a heap before we slept. When Eli woke, he was easier about himself. That day he snowshoed out two times, the next day two more, and brought back the rest of the cached meat. A small part he brought back to me and the rest he left at Fleur's door. As I advised, he made sure she saw him fall to the ground, as burdened with sorrow. Then he rose in a daze and staggered off. He said she had laughed, called after him, asked if hunting down this weak old bull had been too much for him, even though he knew she saw the animal was young, fat and sweet. He was insulted at the scorn in her voice, but I said he should be pleased she spoke at all.

I don't know how to tell this next thing that happened, an event that started baldness in the Pillager women, and added new weight on each side of the feud that would divide our people down the middle, through time. It started with Eli and Sophie. But it spread from the slough to our politics, just like that. The two families ranged on either side of the question of money settlement. I could do nothing. It is embarrassing for a man to admit his arms have thinned, his capacities diminished, and maybe worse than that, his influence over the young of the tribe is gone for good.

I can only tell it step by step.

It began after I left the church with Margaret and you, Lulu. Your grandmother had dragged me to a Benediction Mass where I was greeted by Father Damien.

"Grandfather Nanapush," he smiled, "at last."

"These benches are a hardship for an old man," I complained. "If you had spread them with soft pine-needle cushions, I'd have come before."

Father Damien surveyed the rough pews, and folded his hands inside the sleeves of his robe.

"You must think of their unyielding surfaces as helpful," he offered. "God sometimes enters the soul through the humblest parts of our anatomies, if they are sensitized to suffering."

"A god who enters through the rear door," I countered, "is no better than a thief."

The young helpers gathered and followed the priest as he walked to the altar. I tried to adjust my bones, longing for some comfort, trying not to rustle for fear of Margaret's jabbing elbow. The time was long, and you were never much for church. You wiggled like a squirrel, probed my pockets until you found a bit of hard candy, and put it in your mouth. Your eyes glazed over and you dozed. I felt no great presence either, and decided that the old gods were better, the Anishinabe characters who were not exactly perfect but at least did not require sitting on hard planks.

When Mass was over and the smell of incense was steamed into our clothes, we went out into the starry cold, the snow and stubble fields, and began the long walk home. It was dusk. On either side of us the laden trees were motionless and black. Our footsteps squeaked against the dry snow, the only sound to hear. We spoke very little, and you even ceased singing when the moon rose at half, poised like a balanced cup. We knew the very moment someone else stepped on the road.

We had turned south on the crossroads toward Margaret's,

and the footsteps came unevenly, just out of sight. There were two men by the sound of their feet, one mixed-blood from the drop of his hard bootsoles, the other one, quiet, an Indian. Not long and I heard them talking close behind us. From the backward nonsense of the Indian's language I recognized Boy Lazarre, the one who had spied on Fleur. And the mixed-blood must be Clarence Morrissey. The two stuck together lately because their families had signed the new purchase agreement with the Turcot lumber company, and now spoke in its favor to anyone whom they could collar. They even came to people's houses to beg and argue that this was our one chance, our good chance, that the officials would drop the offer. But wherever Margaret was, she slapped down their words like mosquitoes.

I sensed the bad intent as Boy and Clarence passed us by, and felt that their looks and greetings had an unpleasant edge of excitement. They went on, disappeared in the dark.

"Margaret," I said, "we are going to cut back." My house was close, with no one between us and it, but Margaret wanted to go fetch Nector at her place, and so she kept walking as if she hadn't heard.

I took her arm, caught you and started to turn, but Margaret would have none of this and called me a coward. She grabbed you back to herself. You did not mind getting tossed back and forth between us, laughed, tucked your hand into your grandma's pocket and never missed a step. You had the balance of a mink and you were slippery and clever too, which was good because when the two men jumped out and grappled with us half a mile on, you had the instinct to slip free and dart into the trees.

The two were occupied with Margaret and me at any

rate. We were old enough to snap in two, our bones dry like branches, but we fought as though our enemies were the Nadouissioux kidnappers of our parents' stories. Margaret uttered a war cry that had not been heard for fifty years, and bit Boy Lazarre's hand viciously, giving a wound which would later prove the death of him. As for Clarence, he had all he could do to wrestle me to the ground and knock me half unconscious. When he'd accomplished that, he tied me and tossed me into the wheelbarrow hidden near the road for the purpose of lugging us to the Morrissey barn.

I came to my sense trussed to the center pole, sitting on a pile of hay. Margaret was roped to the cut saplings of a stall across from me, staring straight forward in a rage, a line of froth caught between her lips. All around me tack and harness hung, bright-edged, fragrant with oil. There were a couple of whips I longed to whistle in my hands, but my wrists were bound. On either side of her, shaggy cows chewed cud, shifted their thumping hooves. The air was warm as stew, heavy with their dung. Morrissey had about the only cattle left on the reservation, and two had vanished into a dozen cooking pots since fall. Now this theft gladdened me. I rose by inching along the pole, decided to pierce my ropes against the pointed tines of a pitchfork. I planned on getting Margaret to bite through the ropes that joined my ankles, but the two men came in.

"Children, let us loose," I said, "your game is too rough."

They stood between us, puffed with their secrets.

"Empty old windbag," said Clarence.

"I have a bargain for you." I looked for an opening. "Let us go and we won't tell Pukwan. Boys get drunk sometimes and don't know what they're doing."

Clarence laughed once, hard and loud. "We're not drunk," he said.

"My cousin Pukwan will find you, and have no mercy," I said. "Let us go. I'll sign the papers and get it over with, and I'll convince the old widow."

I signaled Margaret to keep her mouth shut. She blew air into her cheeks but said nothing. Lazarre and Clarence looked at each other and found amusement in what I'd said. I didn't understand until Lazarre slouched and Clarence stood before Margaret, that this had to do with everything. The land purchase. Politics. Eli and Sophie. It was like seeing an ugly design of bruises come clear for a moment and reconstructing the evil blows that made them. Clarence would take revenge for Eli's treatment of his sister by treating Eli's mother in similar fashion. I strained against the ropes.

"You lie when it suits you, skinny old dog," Clarence said, wiping at his lips as if in hunger, anticipating what his mouth would say. "It's her we want, anyhow. We'll shame her and her boys too."

Lazarre raised his fist, swung it casually and tapped my face. It was worse not to be hit full on.

"Easy enough," I said, smooth, "now that you've got her tied. She's plump and good-looking. Eyes like a doe! But you forget that we're together, almost man and wife."

This wasn't true at all, and Margaret's face went rigid with tumbling fury and confusion. I kept talking.

"So of course, if you do what you're thinking, you'll have to kill me afterward, and that will make my cousin Pukwan twice as angry since I owe him a fat payment for a gun which he lent me and I never returned. All the same," I went on—their heads were spinning—"I'll forget you bad boys ever considered such a crime, something so terrible that Father Damien would nail you on boards just like in the example on the wall in church."

Lazarre stopped me in a deadly growl.

"Quit jabbering," said Clarence. "Pukwan's gone off to fight with Pershing in the war. What does he care about you?"

"He won't forget," I countered stubbornly. "He'll come back looking for his money."

But it was like throwing pebbles in a dry lake. "Pukwan's in favor of the sell-off anyway," said Clarence. "He'll come back with his army pay and buy up all you lose." My words left no ripple in the depth of their greed. I saw in Lazarre's face that they intended us great harm, so I tried my last card.

"Whatever you do to Margaret, you are doing to the Pillager woman!" I dropped my voice. "Have you forgotten about Fleur? Don't you know she can think about you hard enough to stop your heart?"

Clarence was too young to be frightened, but he hung on my words in interested expectation. Those same words had a different effect on Lazarre, who dropped his mouth wide open and pointed at his useless tongue. Then he shook himself angrily and drew a razor from his jacket.

"Come near," crooned Margaret, using the old expression. "Let me teach you how to die!"

But she was trapped like a fox and could only hiss her death song over and over while Lazarre stropped the blade with fast vicious movements. Margaret sang shriller, so full of hate that the ropes should have burnt, shriveled, fallen from her body. My struggle set the manger cracking against the barn walls and further confused the cows, who bumped each other and complained. Clarence then sighed, rose, and smashed me. The last I saw before I blacked out, through the tiny closing pinhole of light, was Lazarre approaching Margaret with the blade.

When I woke, minutes later, it was to worse shock. For Lazarre had sliced Margaret's braids clean off and now he was shaving the rest of her scalp. He started almost tenderly at the wide part, and then he pulled the edge down each side of her skull. He did a careful job. He shed not one drop of her blood.

And I could not even speak to curse them. For pressing my jaw down, thick above my tongue, her braids, never cut in this life before, were tied to silence me. Powerless, I tasted their flat, animal perfume.

It wasn't much later, or else it was forever, that we walked out into the night again. We did not speak, but made our way in fierce pain down the road. I was damaged in spirit, more so than Margaret. For now she tucked her shawl over her naked ears and seemed to forget her own bad treatment. She called out in dread each foot of the way, for you. But sharp, bold girl! You had hidden till all was clear and run on to Margaret's house. When we opened the door, we saw you at once, sitting by the stove with Nector, the two of you straight-backed and frightened, then captured with wonder when Margaret slipped off her shawl.

"Where is your hair?" Nector asked in excitement.

I took my hand from my pocket. "Here's what's left of it. I grabbed this when they cut me loose." I was terribly shamed by how pitiful I had been, weak and helpless, but Margaret snatched the two braids from me and coiled them round her fist.

"I knew you would get them, clever man!" she said. There was satisfaction in her voice.

Nector jumped to his feet, a scrawny boy with hair on end. His eyes were round with danger. "Who did that to you, Mama?"

I told him, and he vowed to lie in wait with his brother Eli. But Eli was up north on the trapline now, still trying to prove himself to Fleur. I set the fire blazing. It was strange how kind Margaret was to me, never blaming me or mentioning my embarrassment, saving my pride before the boy. She stowed her braids inside a birchwood box and merely instructed Nector to lay it in her grave, when that time occurred. Then she came near the stove with a broken mirror from beside her washstand, and looked at her image in the cloudy glass.

"My," she pondered, "my." She put the mirror down. "I'll take a knife to them."

And I was thinking too. I was thinking I would have to kill them.

"Nector," I said, "Eli's gone, so you'll have to throw in with me."

He nodded, frowned seriously, still child enough so it was comical to see him imitate a man's method of consideration.

"I'll take my twenty-two," he said.

I told him that was too much of a store-bought revenge to satisfy an oldtime Anishinabe warrior, a man, which he would become when this business was finished. We'd find a method. Yet, I was at a loss to say, right off, how an

116

aching and half-starved grandfather could sensibly attack a young, well-fed Morrissey and a fat, sly Lazarre. Later, I rolled up in blankets in the corner by Margaret's stove and put my mind to the question throughout that night until, exhausted, I fell asleep. I thought of it first thing next morning, too, and still nothing came. It was only after we had some good hot gaulette and walked you back to your mother, that an idea began to grow.

Fleur let us into the cabin, wrapped you in her arms, and then Margaret told what had happened. With a flourish, the old woman took off her scarf and stood bald, eyes burning with unchecked fire. The two women's gazes held. Fleur smoothed the front of her calico shirt, flipped her heavy braids over her shoulders, tapped her finger on the curve of her lips, and then put you down. She walked calmly to the washstand and scraped the edge of her skinning knife keen as glass. Margaret, you, and I watched, did not say a word to make Fleur stop as she cut her braids off, shaved her own head clean, and put the hair in a quilled skin pouch. She turned to us, still beautiful as before, but now in a frightful way. Then she went out, hunting, didn't even bother to wait for night to cover her tracks.

I was going to have to go hunting too.

Though I could wound with pointed jokes, I had never wielded a blade against a human, much less two men. Whoever I missed would kill me, or harm Nector. Not only did I want to protect the boy, but I did not want to die by the lowly hands of Morrisseys. In fact, I didn't think that after Margaret's interesting kindness I wanted to leave this life at all. Her bald head, smooth as an egg, was ridged delicately with bone and gleamed as if it had been polished with a flannel cloth. Maybe it was the strangeness that attracted me. She looked forbidding, but the absence of hair also set off her eyes, so black and full of lights. She did not in the least look pitiful. She looked like that queen from England, like a watersnake or shrewd young bird. And I still tasted the braids in my mouth, smoky and smooth, cool and harsh.

I had better things to do than fight. So I decided to accomplish revenge quick as possible. I was a talker and a hunter who used my brains as my weapon. I decided that I would show Nector how to do that too.

"When I hunt," I said to him as we schemed in my cabin, "I prefer to let my game catch itself."

Nector opened his fingers, snapped them like the steel jaws of his gopher traps. I shook my head. He frowned, at a loss.

"We'll take them to court," he said intensely, slamming his hand on his knee.

"Now you're talking," I said. "You'll make a smooth politician. But our court involves Pukwan's relatives, so here's what I have in mind. Snares. They demand clever fingers and the ability to think exactly like your prey. That requires imagination, and that's the reason snares have never failed me. Snares are quiet, and best of all snares are slow. I'd like to give Lazarre and Morrissey a little time to consider why they have to strangle."

Nector wet his lips.

"Sketch it out here," I invited him. He took a pencil and made his strong fine marks on the edges of my newspaper. One- or two-foot deadfalls were required beneath the snares so that a man couldn't put his hand up and loosen the knot. Snares also required something stronger than a twine, which could be broken, and finer than a rope, which even Lazarre might see and avoid. We had to find the right tree, young and slender, pliable even in the cold. I pondered this closely, yet, even so, we might never have found the answer had I not gone to Mass with Margaret in that interval, and grown curious about the workings of Father Damien's pride and joy, the piano in the back of the church, the instrument whose keys he breathed on, polished, then played after services and sometimes alone at night. I had noticed that, when playing, his hands usually stayed near the middle, so Nector and I cut our wires from either end.

In the meantime, we were not the only ones getting even. Fleur was seen in town. Her thick skirts brushed the snow into clouds behind her. Though it was cold she left her head bare so everyone could see the frigid sun glare off her skull. The light reflected in the eyes of Lazarre and Clarence, who were standing at the door of the pool hall. They dropped their cue sticks in the snow, and ran west to the Morrissey farm, which was so near the settlement. Fleur walked the four streets, once in each direction, then followed.

Clarence later told of her visit, how she stalked through the Morrissey house touching here, touching there, sprinkling powders that ignited and stank on the hot stove. He maintained that had Napoleon or Bernadette or even the two girls been there in the house and not trading off reservation, Fleur might have killed them all with the bad medicine she put together. Clarence told how he had swayed on his feet, blinked hard to look pitiful, and chewed his fingers. How Fleur stepped up to him, drew her razor-sharp knife. He smiled foolishly and asked if she wanted a bite of supper. She reached forward and trimmed off a hank of his hair. Then she swung from the house, leaving a taste of cold wind, and chased Lazarre to the barn. Clarence followed and peered through an unchinked crack.

Fleur made a black silhouette against the light from the door. Lazarre pressed against the wood of the walls, watching, hypnotized at the sight of Fleur's head and the quiet blade. He did not defend himself but his useless tongue clattered when she approached, reached for him, gently and efficiently cut bits of his hair, held his hands and trimmed their nails. She waved the knife before his eyes and swept a few eyelashes into a white square of floursacking that she then carefully folded into her blouse.

For days after, Lazarre babbled and wept. Fleur was murdering him by use of bad medicine. He showed his hand, the bite that Margaret had dealt him, and the dark streak from the wound, along his wrist and inching up his arm.

I figured that the two men were doomed at least three ways now. Margaret won the debate with her Catholic training and swore to damn her soul by taking up the axe, since no one else had destroyed her enemies. I begged her to wait for another week, all during which it snowed and thawed and snowed again. It took us that long to arrange the snare to my satisfaction, near Lazarre's shack, on a path both men took to town.

Nector and I set it out one morning before anyone stirred, then settled in to watch from an old pine twisted along the ground. We waited while the smoke rose in a silky feather from the tin spout on Lazarre's roof. We had to sit half a day before Lazarre came outside, and even then it was just for wood, nowhere near the path. We had a hard time to keep our blood flowing, our stomachs still. I had a harder time than Nector, because I had to take his mind off his cold feet. First I entertained him by calling fox to us, bleating like a rabbit. Then Lazarre poked his head out the door and we gave up that amusement. Nector asked me the questions a small adult might ask, not a boy of nine. He wanted to know how land was parceled out, what sorts of fees were required. We were often worried on this front and Nector took the worry inside himself, more, in fact, than I understood at the time.

"You're not even supposed to think of girls yet," I told him, "let alone an allotment."

"I'm just about a grown man," he informed me, sighting along the blade of his knife.

We ate a handful each of dry berries Margaret had provided us, and doled out a bit of pounded meat. Finally, Clarence showed. He came on fast, never bothered to keep quiet in the woods. Just at the edge of the trees, where we knew he would be scanning forward, checking for trouble or any witness to his visit with Boy, he saw that the signs were clear, surged a little forward, and stepped like a blind ghost into the noose.

It was perfect, or would have been if we had dug the deadfall two inches wider, for in falling Clarence somehow managed to spread his legs and straddle the hole. It had been invisible, covered with thin branches and more snow, and yet in one foot-pedaling instant as he fell, the certain knowledge of its construction sprang into Clarence's brain and told his legs to reach for the sides. I don't know how he did it, but there he was, poised. Nector and I waited, did not move. Wasn't this better than we'd hoped? The noose jerked enough to cut slightly into the fool's neck, a too-snug fit. He was spread-eagled and on tiptoe, his arms extended in straight lines. If he twitched a finger, lost the least control, even tried to yell, one foot would go, the loop constrict.

But Clarence did not move a muscle, stir a hair. He didn't even dare to change the expression on his face. His mouth stayed frozen in shock. Only his eyes shifted, rolled fiercely and wildly, side to side, showing all the agitation he must not release, searching desperately for a way to escape. They only focused when Nector and I stepped toward him, quiet, from the pine.

We were in full view of Lazarre's house, face to face. I motioned Nector to stay in back of me and I stood before Clarence. Just a touch, a sudden kick, perhaps no more than a word was all that it required. But I looked into his eyes and saw the knowledge of his situation.

I said to Nector, "You see this man? He never thought this hard before."

Then pity entered me. Even to erase Margaret's shame, I couldn't do the thing.

We turned away, and left the Morrissey still balanced on the ledge of snow.

You never get a second chance to kill a badger, or a Morrissey either, so I was glad at least that the twisted mouth struck poor Clarence as a reminder. The Morrissey's lip sagged down the left side of his face not long after Lazarre, somehow, contrived to cut him from the tree. Lazarre was so clumsy that the boy half-strangled anyway, trod air, while Lazarre, who favored his throbbing arm, tried to sever the fine strong wire. So perhaps my snare did damage, taught a temporary lesson. The drag of Clarence's mouth was permanent and would announce that he was the cause of the Pillager baldness long after the scars around his neck had whitened.

As for Lazarre himself, the streak on his arm darkened. His fingers weakened and grew numb. He was avoided, though he wandered the streets of town looking for some comfort. I saw him slide away from me a few days after, when I took what money I had and visited the trading store. I bought the costliest bonnet on the shelf, a better one than any woman on the reservation owned. It was black as a coal hod, large, and shaped the same.

"It sets off my doe eyes," Margaret said. From within its arc, she stared me down.

She wore it every day, and at the pre-Lenten Masses. As we walked up the road, voices could be heard. "There goes Old Lady Coalbucket." Nonetheless, she was proud of the hat and softening toward me, I could tell. By the time we got our foreheads crossed with ashes, we were keeping company.

"I hear you're thinking of exchanging the vows," said Father Damien as we shook his hand on our way from the church.

"I'm having relations with Margaret already," I whispered to startle him. "That's the way we do things."

He had dealt with similar problems before, so he was

not even stumped as to what remedy he should use.

"Make a confession, at any rate," he said, motioning me back into the church.

Margaret frowned in suspicion, signaled that she would wait. So I went back indoors and knelt within the little box. Father Damien slid aside the shadowy door. I told him what I had been doing with Margaret and he stopped me partway through.

"No more details. Pray to Our Lady."

"There is one more thing." I took all responsibility, all blame.

"Yes?"

"Clarence Morrissey, he wears a scarf to church around his neck each week. I snared him like a rabbit."

Father Damien let the idea fill him.

"And the last thing," I went on, "I stole the wire from your piano."

The silence spilled over into my stall, and I was held in its grip until the priest spoke.

"Discord is hateful to God. You have offended His ear." Almost as an afterthought, Damien added, "And His commandment. The violence among you must cease."

"You can have the wire back," I said. We had only used one long strand. I also agreed that I would never again use my snares on humans, an easy promise. Lazarre was already caught.

Just two days later, while your mother and I were showing six quill baskets to the trader, looking for a price, Lazarre entered the store. His eyes rolled to the skull when he saw Fleur. He stretched forth his arm and pointed along its deepest black vein and dropped his jaw wide. Then he stepped backward into a row of traps that the trader had set to show us how they worked. Your mother's eye lit, her white scarf caught the sun as she turned. All the whispers were true. She had scratched Lazarre's figure into a piece of birchbark, drawn his insides, and rubbed a bit of vermilion up his arms until the red stain reached his heart. There was no sound as he fell, no cry, no word, and the traps of all types that clattered down around his body jumped and met for a long time, snapping air.

The snow came down and closed the roads. My traps yielded nothing and even the gophers went deep underground and disappeared. The nuns at the Mission lived off only bread. What they saved by going hungry all week was given to the children whose parents carried them to Holy Mass.

Every night, Margaret axed off a little wedge of the frozen moose meat and boiled it for me. We drank brews of whatever she could cut in the woods—pin cherry, slippery elm. We sent Nector out to the trapline to live with Eli, in a winter camp, where they'd be sure to snare a rabbit or trap a muskrat. The snow continued, our moose gave out, and Margaret began to work on me.

"Let's live at my place, my cellar is full of jars."

"Go get them then."

But Margaret refused to unseal the trapdoor in her kitchen, or remove her canning from the underground shelves where those jars belonged. I told her she was trying to starve me from my place, that if she wanted what I gave her every night, she better stay.

"Frostbite," she muttered. "The selfish old man pulls the covers from me."

Although the opposite was true, I pretended not to hear and she used a louder tone.

"We might as well live inside a log fence," she pointed out. "The wind gathers strength passing through the cracks of these walls."

"Then stuff something into them," I urged.

She glared at me from the wings of the bonnet she did not remove, some nights, even when she got into bed beside me.

"What's there to stuff!"

She swept around the cabin, grabbing our poor few blankets and extra clothes. She opened my third wife's trunk, and then I leaped up and caught her arm.

"Drop them," I ordered, but she snatched the precious scraps of bedding and embroidered shawls to herself, then slipped outside. I heard the sounds of ripping material a moment later. I flew out after her and stood before her, threw my arm in the air, held my walking stick high and then froze in this mistaken and terrible pose. For she had torn her own skirt to mend the crack, as she showed triumphantly, and was not the least bit frightened by my threat.

"Strike!" she goaded. "Next time the snow thaws I'll be in town, telling how poor Nanapush has lost the use of every other stick, except his cane!"

"Liar!" I put my arm down. "I've exhausted you, admit the truth."

"I've fallen asleep," she said, "if that's what you mean."

I went too far then. "A prickly-headed woman takes what she can find!"

Her eyes darkened with victory. I'd left an opening for her knife. She first threw down the blankets and the shawls, treasures from my past. Then she reminded me of who was tied beside her, helplessly, who watched as Lazarre stropped his razor. She reminded me of how I lost the respect of others, lost my manhood, of how fortunate I was to have a woman who would overlook such shame.

I turned away.

"Better if they'd cut my throat," I muttered, "or your tongue."

She turned the other way, began to walk, and it was weeks before I saw her again.

Without her presence, there was little to remind me what life was good for. I got too lazy to feed myself, let the last potatoes rot, then I became too weak to set new traps in the woods. To dull my stomach pains, I did not search for food, instead I smoked red willow. I began to fall asleep in the middle of my reading. Then one day I could not rise from my blankets, my limbs weak as water, and I dreamed the dream I had in those days after my family was taken.

I stood in a birch forest of tall straight trees. I was one among many in a shelter of strength and beauty. Suddenly, a loud report, thunder, and they toppled down like match-sticks, all flattened around me in an instant. I was the only one left standing. And now, as I weakened, I swayed and bent nearer to the earth.

It took Margaret one hour to revive me when the snow ceased, and her anger had turned to worry. She forced into my mouth a spoon of last summer's berries, and with that taste the sweetness of those days came back. I had not been certain those times would come again. Hunger steals the memory. I sniffed the air and smelled a soup Margaret had boiled from bones she carried in her pocket. I opened my eyes to see you, assigned to watch my face for movement. Your grandmother stepped forward, the great black bonnet on her head, and put the new-baked gaulette into my hands. I watched my fingers tear the bread, pinch the crust. I felt the brush of the soft crumbs on my lips, but I tasted nothing. The inside of my mouth had lost sense out of disuse. Still, I could feel the bread go down each time I chewed and swallowed, which I did until I'd made a heavy ball inside my middle.

With that, I felt better.

You stood before me, proud, anxious that I notice the pair of shoes tied to your belt. They were thin patent leather dance shoes, costly-looking, bright.

"Where did they come from?" I asked.

Margaret pursed her lips, but spoke proudly. "Eli. He went out with his mink dog the other day. He saw a trail where those mink tried to hide inside a muskrat house, and trapped them that same afternoon. The trader gave him twenty dollars. You want to know what he brought to our doorstep? A fifty pound flour, these shoes, a blanket for me. And this."

She gave me a box of shells.

"Those shoes are too fancy though," said Margaret, "so we tied them onto Lulu's sash."

You twirled to show off the slippers, attached by slender straps to your leggings and wool skirt. You were bundled so tight you looked fat, though your face was pale and shrunken.

"You shouldn't waste any food on a weak old man," I

said to Margaret. "Or a foolish one, or a stupid one. I burned up my cane."

Between the curved sides of the bonnet, her cheeks revealed shadows. Her skin was dry and through it I could see the outlines of her sharp skull, her arching brow. I felt sorrow to notice this, and me so helpless. So I marveled.

"Who would think that a coalbucket could make a woman look so delicious?"

She turned away and busied herself, but I could tell that she was pleased.

Later that night, and many nights after, till I got well enough to travel out to Matchimanito where we would all live together to conserve on our travel and our food, Margaret made you a nest of blankets near the stove and lay down on the bed with me. Our talk floated upward in the darkness, swirled around the past and the present. I knew the breaths and nights we had left were numbered, but I was too weak to make any hay. I said to her, "Maybe I'm ruined for it, after all."

Margaret laughed though.

"As long as your voice works, the other will."

Eli left the scarf of fine white woven cloth with Fleur for days before he dared follow it to her hands. He finally opened the door to her cabin, stepped in. I don't know if he kept his head hung down, as I counseled, if he fell to his knees and clutched Fleur's skirt to dry the tears from his eyes, if he used the gesture that had softened the heart of my White Beads, so long ago.

Whatever he did worked, and things improved, we heard.

. . .

That winter, holes were chopped in Matchimanito and our people fished with no concern for the lake man down there, no thought but food. People stood on ice for hours, waiting, slapping themselves, with nothing to occupy them but their hunger and their children's hunger. It was natural that to take their minds off their own problems, they would cast their eyes to shore and learn a thing or two about what was happening with Fleur Pillager and Eli Kashpaw.

It was worth their watch.

The chimney of the Pillager place smoked day and night, but no person was seen in the yard. Faint calls were heard, unmistakably human, thin in the freezing sky, uncontained by the thick walls of the cabin. These cries were full of pleasure, strange and wonderful to hear, sweet as the taste of last summer's fruit. Bundled in strips of blanket, coats stuffed with leaves and straw, our people pushed their fur caps and scarves from their ears and drifted out of their wind shields of pine branch, drawn along the ice. Sounds carried so well through the hollow air, even laughing whispers, that people stood fast, let the chill reach deep into their bones, until they heard the satisfaction of silence. Then they turned away and crept back with hope. Faintly warmed, they leaned down to gather in their icy lines.

Spring 1918–Winter 1919
Payaetonookaedaed-geezis
Wood Louse Sun

—

P A U L I N E

I had starved myself for so long that I had no way of knowing, when I first felt the movement, how far back to count. So I did not know when I would bear it. And since I had already betrothed myself to God, I tried to force it out of me, to punish, to drive it from my womb. Bernadette caught me out back of the house one afternoon, pushing the handle of an axe against my stomach. But though I fell upon the wooden pole again and again, till I was bruised, Napoleon's seed had too strong a hold.

"That's no good!" Bernadette rushed to me and pinned my arms. She kicked the axe away and held me close until I ceased in the struggle and fell against her. In my half-faint, I felt the strong boards of her chest, the sweaty fragrance of her like a horse, and her goodness. I knew she would not assist me, not unless I raised her anger.

"Don't whip me!" I wept. "Don't even wonder! It was Napoleon."

Her arms tightened, flat ribbons of muscle and sinew, and she said the thing for which I had no use.

"I'll take the child." She let me go, bowed her head, and sat on the woodpile, resting her cheeks in the cup of her hands.

"No," I said.

She lifted her face, understood.

"Help me," I whispered, "surely you know . . ."

"That's a mortal sin."

She rose, swung the axe overhead, and brought it down clean and hard so it stuck in the block without a quiver.

After that we made a plan together to hide the fact of my condition. We were both clever with materials and scissors, and between us we devised a concealing dress that would allow me to accompany Bernadette until I became too advanced. Once that happened, I would not venture off the farm. She would deliver me, having knowledge in her hands of birth as well as death. But there was one firm condition that she made: that I must not try again to do away with the child. I promised, but it was harder than you might think to ignore the ideas that crept into my mind. I knew that Moses Pillager, who had given me the love charm, helped out the girls upon whom it worked too well. He concocted medicines of pounded roots and barks. If I had known them I would have purged my own body. I thought of cinching my stomach with tight ropes, or jumping off the roof. Only Bernadette's constant and assessing looks,

132

only the spoonfuls of lumpy soup she forced down me, only the bed she made from then on at the foot of her own, kept my promise.

I even knew the sex of it, the name.

Marie, she said, named for the Virgin. I knew different. Satan was the one who had pinned me with his horns.

And as it grew, or *she* grew, she punched with her powerful head and rolled and twisted like an otter. When she did this, the fits of hate took me so hard that I wept, dug my sharp fingernails into the wood of the table.

Bernadette's other command was that Napoleon not show his face to me. She put his clothes, his fiddle, his moccasins and his hard Sunday shoes out in the barn and barred the house to him. Clarence was the messenger, the go-between, the one who brought Napoleon the food plate that Bernadette filled and put on the sill. From the window of the upstairs room I watched him eat, his chair an old elm stump in the yard. Hunched over, he shoveled the flat of the knife to his mouth. He wiped his plate clean with bread and then smoked a roll-up cigarette or two, after which he fetched the fiddle. He played French rounds and jigs in the floating dusk. That music, the saws and screams, the relentless dark cheerfulness a bludgeon through the walls, went on and on until my ears stung and I felt that they would fly off my head.

Sophie ran outside to dance with Philomena. They twisted and hopped in each other's arms, dodged around Napoleon's absorption. They grew thinner and wilder while I grew large. The skin on my stomach tightened to a white transparency. Through that parchment, I tried to read the child. She moved less now, hemmed in and held. I thought I could bear it if only she would come soon. Yet I continued to expand, a risen loaf that birth would punch down. I hoped, I prayed to be delivered.

But that did not happen.

Summer fled and all the living plants dried to stalk and seed. The earth hardened. I swelled so tight that I could hardly lift my arms and every breath was forced, fought for against her weight. I felt my bones give, the bowl of my hips creak wide, and between my legs there was a soft and steady burning.

Bernadette put me to bed and told me not to move. From the window, I watched the men gather in the last of the wheat with a hired contraption that pounded and rattled and shot steam into the air so that I could neither rest nor keep, in my mind, a steady prayer. And then later, off through the dead fields, I heard the wild and raucous clanging of armistice bells that went on and on all day until I screamed at the noise, which brought no peace to me.

Although my baby arrived then, as if at their signal.

Words were useless. Thoughts foolish. All of the mind's constructions. Time passed slowly because the pain was predictable, fast because it was a brimming well. I was slapped by a great beast, thrown over its shoulder, shaken like a child in the grip of its mother. I marveled at the breath torn out of me. I heard my own cries. Bernadette's voice bloomed and faded in my ear, telling me to do things, where to put my legs, when to suffer the humiliations of her touch. She instructed me to hold my breath or release, and finally, to push the child out with all my remaining strength.

But by then I had gained too much understanding, plunged too many times, seen too far.

One branch flared out the window, the tip of a tree, so alone in the grinding darkness. If I gave birth, I would be lonelier. I saw, and I saw too well. I would be an outcast, a thing set aside for God's use, a human who could be touched by no other human. Marie! I shook with the effort, held back, reduced myself to something tight, round, and very black clenched around my child so that she could not escape. I became a great stone, a boulder set under a hill.

"Push, help me," Bernadette cried.

I dug my heels into the sheets, into the straw ticking, shut and held. But the child moved, inched forward. Her will was stronger. I sat up suddenly and gripped the top rails of the bed. I deceived her, lay sideways, and let the convulsions of her movements pass.

"Little fool!" Bernadette was beside herself with fear, with anger, and now we struggled. I held still and howled and in the interludes I told Bernadette I had decided to die, and let the child too, no taint of original sin on her unless she breathed air.

Bernadette did not slap my face or argue in temper. She firmed her lips. She left, and I thought in confusion maybe she'd abandoned us. But soon she came back into the room with a coil of rope. She also brandished an instrument made of two black iron cooking spoons, wired together at the handles. These she laid on the bed. She tied my arms to the rails, then spread my legs and tied them by the ankles to the bedstead underneath the mattress. I was roped in place as tight as she could pull. And when the next pains, and the next, and the next pains threw me upwards, straining at the bindings, she managed to put the spoons to the child's head and wrench her into the world.

We were divided.

The light was concentrated in one corner, the child was crying. I could hear her high scratching bawl, an inconsolable tune. I looked upon her. She was soiled, formed by me, bearing every defilement I had known by Napoleon Morrissey. The spoons had left a dark bruise on both temples.

"Look," I said. "She's marked by the devil's thumbs."

"No, she's not," said Bernadette. "Take her. Put her to your breast."

But the child was already fallen, a dark thing, and I could not bear the thought. I turned away.

"You keep Marie."

She did. And I left that house when I could walk.

At the convent, I arose before the rest of them each morning. In that cold dark hour, the air stiff as iron, I made the fire, broke the crusts of ice off the buckets of water, then set them boiling for laundry, for the breakfast soup, for washing, for all else that would take place once we'd finished morning prayer.

The stove was larger than any I'd ever seen, and although our wood was chopped by a team of devout men, there was never enough to keep it stoked. My pallet, which I rolled small each morning and hid, was cold even though I slept with my back against the firebox. All winter, my blood never thawed. My stomach never filled. My hands were chafed raw. And yet I grew strong. My shoulders hardened and I gained in height. I could kneel hour upon hour. It was no punishment to me.

"Accept this," I asked Him when night after night the

cold gripped me in tight claws and I shook so hard I could not sleep. "And this," every time I sat to eat and halved my bread. When my stomach pinched, "This also, my Lord." When the blood rushed back into my frozen hands after taking the sheets off the line, "This too. This. And this."

And He did. I grew in knowledge. Skins were stripped from my eyes. Every day I saw more clearly and I marveled at what He showed me.

For instance, exactly where I was from.

One night of deepest cold He sat in the moonlight, on the stove, and looked down at me and smiled in the spill of His radiance and explained. He said that I was not whom I had supposed. I was an orphan and my parents had died in grace, and also, despite my deceptive features, I was not one speck of Indian but wholly white. He Himself had dark hair although His eyes were blue as bottleglass, so I believed. I wept. When He came off the stove, his breath was warm against my cheeks. He pressed the tears away and told me I was chosen to serve.

Other things. I was forgiven of my daughter. I should forget her. He had an important plan for me, for which I must prepare, that I should find out the habits and hiding places of His enemy. It was only very slowly that this idea was revealed. Over time, as winter cut down more people and I was called from the convent to house after house where I prepared the newly dead, the details of His great need were given. I should not turn my back on Indians. I should go out among them, be still, and listen. There was a devil in the land, a shadow in the water, an apparition that filled their sight. There was no room for Him to dwell in so much as a crevice of their minds.

"The Indians," I said now, "them." Never *neenawind* or us. And I soon found it was good that I did. For one day during supper Sister Anne announced that Superior had received word that our order would admit no Indian girls, and that I should go to her and reveal my true background. Which I did. And Superior said she was delighted that the hindrance was removed, since it was plain to see that I abided in His mystical body. She had never known a novice so serious and devoted, or so humble. I swelled on that and smiled.

"Dear Mother," I said in a soft voice, "I am small."

Her mouth twitched to see me kneeling there, a coarse hulk of bones.

"At least in regard to your soul." But then she pondered. "I do think many times of The Little Flower, when I see you. Tell me. Does Our Lord ever answer when you pray?"

I considered telling everything, but feared she would misunderstand. Like the tears of Our Blessed Lady, which had melted on my skirt, His plans for me could not be completely explained or proved. So the visit was all that I shared.

"He comes in the dark. He sits on the stove and talks to me," I said.

She did not answer.

"He doesn't stay long though, Mother. He says it is much too cold."

She was quiet for a good while, then she said, "We'll have to welcome Him at night then, by burning a few extra sticks."

I spent a week in the woods with a sled, collecting deadwood, in order to pay for my impudence. But she did have mercy and allowed me to stoke the stove once before sleep so the warmth should linger. She gave me her own thin blanket, though I'm certain she wore her own fine woolen cloak to sleep. If she did toss, seeking warmth, it would have been a terrible penance for my sake. I was tempted to relieve her mind, to tell her that my preservation was worth discomfort. I was tempted to tell her the truth. But as I was on the verge of it, I noticed that my own shadow moved when I did not, which was often how Satan revealed himself, pressed so close. Then I knew the dark one had whispered that thought in my ear and I resisted. I did not tell Superior, or return her blanket, but waited for the light, for the next instruction by His lips, as to what I should do about Fleur.

She was the one who closed the door or swung it open. Between the people and the gold-eyed creature in the lake, the spirit which they said was neither good nor bad but simply had an appetite, Fleur was the hinge. It was like that with Him, too, Our Lord, who had obviously made the whites more shrewd, as they grew in number, all around, some even owning automobiles, while the Indians receded and coughed to death and drank. It was clear that Indians were not protected by the thing in the lake or by the other Manitous who lived in trees, the bush, or spirits of animals that were hunted so scarce they became discouraged and did not mate. There would have to come a turning, a gathering, another door. And it would be Pauline who opened it, same as she closed the Argus lockers. Not Fleur Pillager.

One night I saw.

They were moving. It was as old Nanapush had said when we sat around the stove. As a young man, he had guided a buffalo expedition for whites. He said the animals understood what was happening, how they were dwindling.

He said that when the smoke cleared and hulks lay scattered everywhere, a day's worth of shooting for only the tongues and hides, the beasts that survived grew strange and unusual. They lost their minds. They bucked, screamed and stamped, tossed the carcasses and grazed on flesh. They tried their best to cripple one another, to fall or die. They tried suicide. They tried to do away with their young. They knew they were going, saw their end. He said while the whites all slept through the terrible night he kept watch, that the groaning never stopped, that the plains below him was alive, a sea turned against itself, and when the thunder came, then and only then, did the madness cease. He saw their spirits slip between the lightning sheets.

I saw the same. I saw the people I had wrapped, the influenza and consumption dead whose hands I had folded. They traveled, lame and bent, with chests darkened from the blood they coughed out of their lungs, filing forward and gathering, taking a different road. A new road. I saw them dragging one another in slings and litters. I saw their unborn children hanging limp or strapped to their backs, or pushed along in front hoping to get the best place when the great shining doors, beaten of air and gold, swung open on soundless oiled fretwork to admit them all.

Christ was there, of course, dressed in glowing white.

"What shall I do now?" I asked. "I've brought You so many souls!"

And He said to me, gently:

"Fetch more."

Which is what I intended by going out among them with the net of my knowledge. He gave me the mission to name and baptize, to gather souls. Only I must give myself away in return, I must dissolve. I did so eagerly. I had nothing to leave behind, and nothing to acquire, either, except what would come into His hands. I fit easily through the eye of a needle. And once I had passed to the other side I made my way to the Pillager cabin.

From the outside, I could not tell if they suffered. The logs were tightly tamped and the roof secured on squarely. Woodsmoke poured from the chimney into cold still air. I walked to the door and lightly rapped. I was dressed as a novice now, in gaiters and thick gray woolens. My hair was partly hidden, a cross of myrtlewood hung from my neck, and my waist was belted by a forged metal rosary.

Fleur opened the door, looked at me and laughed. Her face was starved lean. Her hair was covered by a white scarf and her silver earrings burned in the sun. Although very slender, she was surviving. Maybe she had a squash or two stored in the root cellar, or a bag of potatoes, or maybe it was Eli. Some said he was back and some said he had disappeared. Perhaps he knew how to find the last of the game in the woods.

"You turned holy," Fleur said, and put her fingers to her lips. She was dressed in a dark wool blouse, a skirt heavy as a blanket, and her shoulders were wrapped in a shawl of brown yarn. She carried the unborn baby low.

"May I enter?"

She turned her face, starkly boned, set off by white cloth, into the dim space of the cabin and raised her brows at someone else. "This Morrissey comes knocking at my door," she said.

"I'm no Morrissey," I said in wonder, then stepped past her, over the threshold and onto the floor of pressed dirt that Fleur had swept and strewed with hides. I removed my thin-soled boots and took a place near the stove.

"You wouldn't have a little scrap to eat..." I said to Fleur. I fought to control my voice. This was what He meant. Humility. I turned and nodded to the man in the shadows, Eli Kashpaw. He made not the slightest move to acknowledge my greeting. Fleur did not stir either, not toward the kettle of water, not toward the cupboard. She folded her arms inside the shawl and drew it close.

"And now this girl begs."

I put my hands in my lap. Who could tell what they knew or did not know? What rumors?

"I have no family," I said, in His guidance. "I am alone and have no land. Where else would I go but to the nuns?"

Fleur and Eli were silent. A mound of covers tossed on the bed. It was Lulu, curled up inside like a mouse, dreaming in fits.

"If only your child never has to know my suffering!" Under their strict indifference I felt sorry for myself. "You were the only ones good to me."

"Not true," said Fleur, "there were the Morrisseys." She took off her scarf and showed her prickly scalp.

I had been stupid. I did not think blame for the shaving would fall upon me.

"I got quit of those Morrisseys!" I said. Fleur tied the scarf on tightly. "Or at least all except for Bernadette. I went to the convent because I couldn't stand those men." Then inspiration struck. I lowered my voice.

"Napoleon, the old drunk, tried to have his way with me, beat me and knocked me down in the barn. I left because I couldn't fend him off forever."

Fleur searched my face with her hard narrow eyes, and then amusement welled up in her and she turned away to smile at Eli, who pretended to be occupied with the repair of a cooking pot.

"You find something funny in that." I made my voice tremble.

"I was just remembering your new little cousin," Fleur smoothly said, "the one Bernadette took home, a child of your relative. It's a quick little baby, agile and strong. But it doesn't look like a Christian."

"I know nothing about her," I said too quickly, "tell me."

"You know she's a girl." Fleur smiled. "She has a Puyat mouth, turned down at the corners. Except hers hasn't told any lies."

Still, Fleur forgave me, left an unguarded spot to attack. She allowed me to stay in the warmest chair and fed me bannock. But perhaps she was only tired, more concerned with all the ones she had to care for, her daughter, Lulu, Margaret, even that old pagan Nanapush.

As for him, I had to bear such torment.

If he was there in those winter days when I came to visit, he tried to lift my habit with his walking stick and glimpse what I wore beneath. He also wanted to see my hairshirt, insisted on it no matter how many times I denied I wore one. But at last, in a distracted moment, I confessed that I had made a set of underwear from potato sacks, and when I wore it the chafing reminded me of Christ's sacrifice. This delighted him, encouraged him. He was curious to know how the undergarments were sewed, if I had to take them off to perform the low functions. He suggested after mock-serious thought that I might secretly enjoy the scratch of the rough material against my thighs.

"Like the beard of a Frenchman," I thought I heard him mumble.

I spoke high and loud. "Suffering is a gift to God! I have given away everything I owned. All that I have left is my body's comfort and pleasure, and I give that last pearl to Him now."

"A pearl without any price," Nanapush agreed, or disagreed, leaning on his stick. His long white hair was wrapped in red ties, and his face was seamed and polished. He had a hawk nose and wide high cheekbones, aged into knobs. His wide mouth was withered from lack of teeth and he was bent, but it was easy to imagine he had once been as fine-looking as people said, with a way of satisfying wives. He smiled his gapped smile.

"And what about the fruit without price?" he soon wondered. "Did you give that up too?"

I was stern. "You mean Christ. He dwells within us, He is the fruit of the Virgin's womb."

"No," he said, leaning toward me with a false frown. "Not that fruit. The cherry."

I pretended not to understand the lumberjack and whiskey-trade slang Nanapush had picked up in his life.

"Quit this talk," Margaret said sharply, poised behind the old man's chair, wielding her spoon. She was devout enough not to allow teasing on church matters in her vicinity. But the fiend would not be silenced.

"I don't see," he said, "getting back to pearls . . ."

Margaret seemed to know what he was driving at.

"An old man's pearls pester him. We know." She cuffed at him with the spoon and turned away, adjusting the black bonnet that she wore even under the roof.

He called after her.

"They pester all right, these large firm onions. They make me weep."

When she turned back she had a plate in her hand, stew made from a winter grouse that was all bones. The soup was shredded meat, marrow, and some cattail roots, boiled. It scented the room, called to the body with its fragrance, even though it was mainly water.

"We might as well boil sticks," Margaret said, setting it in front of Nanapush.

She dished the next plate to Eli, then one to Fleur, who halved hers with Lulu. There was a small bit left over which she gave to me. I drank it down before I saw that she had taken none for herself.

Nanapush handed his nearly full plate back to Margaret, who took a spoonful and passed the dish to Fleur, whose bowl was already cleaned by Lulu.

"I ate while I cooked," said Margaret. She looked at Fleur, so gaunt, the baby pushing out, and at Lulu, eating with such ravenous attention, sucking the thin bones and licking her fingers. "We old ones don't need much, because our stomachs are too bitter."

Nanapush was sly enough to get the better of me sometimes by asking questions without limit or end. He waylaid me when I walked past his house on the way to a sickness, or cornered me when I visited at the Pillagers'. No one defended me, although they were usually polite enough. It was as if they had realized by some instinct what the Lord told me from His throne on the front burner of the stove. They treated me as they would a white. I was ignored most of the time. When they did address me they usually spoke English.

They also shared the old man's secret jokes.

One afternoon Nanapush was there when I entered, and of course he noticed the ingenious reminder of Christ's imprisonment I had devised, that of wearing my shoes on the wrong feet.

He gestured downward with his little smoking pipe.

"God is turning this woman into a duck," he said.

Everyone was immediately caught by that, and curious. I tucked my feet beneath my habit but Lulu, of course, kept close watch and stared down with excitement whenever I moved. Walking was a great deal more uncomfortable and difficult than one might suppose. My inner foot ached, I lurched, wore painful sores into my skin. I had to hide these marks from the other nuns. But whenever I was tempted to put the shoes on the proper way I recalled Christ's last journey to my mind, His bare feet on the cobbled stones, and the nail holes through them.

"Accept this," I prayed inwardly, when Nanapush jabbed and laughed at my stumbling shuffle. One day, he shot dart after dart of foolish questions and overcame my resistance.

"Did Jesus wear his sandals on the wrong feet?"

"No, He didn't."

"Then why do you?"

"I suffer for His sake as He did for yours," I said. "I miswear my shoes for mortification." I did not add that I followed this practice only when away from the convent, as Superior discouraged my unusual penances.

Nanapush was silent, as if in meditation, then he spoke. "You are like no one else." His manner was, for once, serious and thoughtful. I could detect not a hint of hidden scorn. He pondered. "Maybe you are the most unusual woman I know."

It was foolish to feel a glimmer of hope in his direction, but he was old, and perhaps his soul was ready to be plucked. I should at least try to add it to my wealth.

I said simply, "Some are called."

"That's exactly right," said Nanapush, knocking his cane upon the floor in sudden enthusiasm, "that is why you are so different. I have observed it."

I allowed myself to feel demure. My pride was overwhelmingly tempted.

"What have you observed, Uncle?" I asked.

"This," said Nanapush intensely. "You never have to answer the call."

"Oh yes," I said, confused, "I must answer His every word!"

"Then he must never call you to relieve yourself."

I gaped. He said this last to me in the old language, and the words were strong and vulgar.

"I have noticed," he continued, "that you sit here all day and never visit the outhouse."

It was true, and I was shamed and I was furious. The toothless ruin had discovered my most secret practice, which was to allow myself only two times of the day for that function, dawn and dusk. No one noticed in the convent. No one reported, as they had when I left the pins in my headpiece and when I wore a short length of rope around my neck, reminding me not to betray my Lord as Judas had.

"You filthy mouth," I said, my tongue loose and unbridled. "I hope the devil tears you apart piece by piece and fries each morsel!"

He looked horrified, apologized at once, made a sick, meek face and slunk out the door, which was so unlike him that I thought perhaps I'd been unrighteous, harsh. But, as it happened, I should have gone farther and done worse, for he lay in wait and lulled me for a week. He watched for the right moment.

I came from a sickbed one afternoon, and had not drunk anything all day so I could last the final hours. I found it difficult, after midday repast, to put my mind for long on anything but dusk's consolation and release. I kept myself calmed while the sun was out, through deep prayer and furious concentration. I had good reason. He had hinted that I might gain eternal life if I never broke my pact and paid the privy an extra visit. It was a hard yoke that I accepted, but I hadn't yet failed. However, I was seduced by Nanapush's false kindness, for he had brewed a special pot of strong sassafras and mixed sugar into it.

Sugar. How we all craved the taste.

The weather was cold and threatening. The cabin was warm, the air humid with the fragrance of the rich bronze bark Nanapush had gathered and boiled. A soup was cooking too, some muskrat and corn, that brought tears of longing to my eyes. I sipped the tea. The sweet hot mixture left an unbearable thrill in my mouth. The watch had been long, I hadn't slept, and the wonderful comfort of sugar made me dreamy. I listened halfheartedly to Margaret tell some story about the way things used to happen with the people in their clan. Before I knew it, the first cup was gone, and then the second, and then I just kept drinking and listening. At some point Nanapush took over talking. It was still light out, the dusk about two hours hence. I had become good at calculating winter afternoons. I was gaining fortitude for summer, when the sun set late.

"My story is this," said Nanapush. "There was once a little rain. It fell on a girl's head a drop at a time."

I pushed my cup away regretfully. I was uncomfortable and realized I must stop. The old man continued.

"The rain got stronger. It began to fall in lines. You know how water hisses down on the lake. It fell like that. It fell and fell. More rain. Then that girl began to float. She was in a deep flood that dragged her all around the earth until she saw something sticking out of the waves. She swam over and clung to it."

Margaret laughed. Fleur was drowsily listening, curled against Eli. Lulu was crouched on the old man's knees. The light seemed brighter outside, unfading. I cursed all the talk of water and began a rosary in my thoughts. But I saw the sorrowful mystery, Christ in Gethsemane. He wept a river, and I could not keep from hearing the voice of Nanapush. In the old language there are a hundred ways to describe water and he used them all—its direction, color, source and volume.

"The sticking-out thing spoke to the girl, and said if it kept sticking out and saved her, she must do what it wanted afterward. And she agreed."

"Of course she did," said Margaret, extending her arms for Lulu. "Come over here my girl." She tried to distract the child, but Lulu was listening, bright with interest.

"The water rose," said Nanapush.

His voice was so light that I glanced at him in suspicion, but he appeared to be completely involved in his story.

"It crept up her ankles, then got to her knees. It lapped

higher, higher, under her skirt. Then it was up to her waist."

I was unpleasantly affected, and tapped my feet to divert myself. As the water in the story mounted, my feet jigged the harder.

"A wonder," said Nanapush, stopping all of a sudden. "This duck can jitterbug!"

"Have more tea to calm yourself," said Margaret.

But I went rigid and did not relax control even of my voice.

"The water," said Nanapush, "soon covered her breasts, then rose slowly, higher, to her chin. There it stopped."

"And went back down," said Margaret, forgetting Lulu, "surely we know this! All the way down until the sticking-up thing was exposed."

Nanapush made as if to unbutton his pants. Eli laughed in the corner, and Fleur boldly urged him on. Margaret hid Lulu's eyes, but Lulu threw her hand off.

"It belonged to my ancestor," said Nanapush, "and now it was time for the girl to act as they had agreed..." He leaned toward me, whispered as if to keep the child from hearing. "So they coupled until their parts smoked."

I stared at my fists. I did not dare move and now knew the tea, the story, were his plan. He was informed by Satan, sent to me on purpose to test my resolve. He meant to bar me from gaining joy in the presence of my Savior, in heaven where I would be finished with such earthly humiliations as I suffered now with each corner of my mind, each muscle. I strained to make myself into a block of ice. To think of droughted fields and dust on the road. To think of Him and of His special love for martyrs. I whispered rosaries underneath my breath to block the words of Nanapush. But

I couldn't block the sight of what he pulled from his vest.

"Nine months later," he said, "a little boy came into the world."

Between his fingers, he was holding what the men down in Argus called a safety. He began to fill it with sassafras tea, from the spout. Before my eyes, the thin skin elongated and ballooned. I was sick. I began to shake all over, groaned deep in my chest.

"It was the child of the flood and was nothing but water," said Nanapush. "Time passed and the boy grew and grew. His skin got tighter."

Nanapush poured more tea.

The others howled and rocked. Wet tears rolled down my cheeks. The safety swelled horribly. Life forever! Eternal peace! I tried to keep my mind stern and pure.

Then the skin burst and a wave poured across the table under Margaret's amused scolding.

I said a thousand prayers in one drenched second. I made for the door in a crouching run and didn't care if I failed in the test, or even if I had to suffer a million years of the devil's laughter, just so I could relieve my burden.

The old man's false quaver rang in my ears. "You have to dry a soaked potato sack in sunlight! Come back! Listen to an old man. I'm only telling this for your benefit!"

How many days of purgatory? How many days of joy? God measured the latter with a teaspoon into my life. At the convent my hands cracked. The knuckles were tight and scabbed. My routine was both simple to follow and terribly hard, as I set new limits. At night, I did not allow myself to toss or turn for comfort, but only to sleep on my back, arms crossed on my breasts in the same position as the Virgin received the attentions of our Lord. When I woke I released myself, and then broke the ice on the buckets. I used my hand and no spoon. I drank only hot water, took the thinnest cut of bread unless Superior forced hers on me. I could not refuse her gift and thereby steal a jewel from the kingdom of her soul. I put burrs in the armpits of my dress and screwgrass in my stockings and nettles in my neckband. Superior forced me to turn my shoes the right way around, but I let my toenails grow until it ached to walk again and each step reminded me of His tread on the path to Calvary. And also, because He asked, I did not give up my purpose.

Some saints endured burning pitch or redhot tongs. Some were torn asunder by lions or, like Perpetua, exposed to a mad heifer that flourished its hooves. There was Cecilia, who outlived her own beheading, and Saint Blaise, combed to death with an iron rake. Saint John of the Cross was shut in a closet for a year, and half devoured by his own lice. Saint Catherine whirled. Predictable shapes, these martyrdoms. Mine took another form.

Embarrassment. I counseled myself to suffer Nanapush. If the history is written of my endurance, let it report that I never toppled, never gave way to fury, but tried with gentle patience to hoist his soul out of the slop pail. To do this, it was necessary to accept his jabs and arrows. The potato sacks I wore beneath my woolen gown were malodorous, I know. Nanapush pinched his nose shut and howled when I arrived at Fleur's house one day.

"Get them off and dry them in the sun like I told you!"

The cold was deep, sharp as bones, but even so he refused me entrance to the Pillager cabin.

"Go, go!" he said. "You're more and more like the whites who never wash themselves clean!"

It was one of my penances, not washing, for it is a sweet vanity to have a pleasant smell. However, God makes no distinction. He would rather have a good soul that stank like a cheese then a bad soul fragranced with rose oil and myrrh. My rank aroma was the perfume my soul exuded, devotion's air.

"Oh let her in," Fleur said from inside, her voice tired. "I'll boil some water." I heard the clanging of pans.

"Those drawers of hers will fall apart string by rotten string," Nanapush muttered. He glared, donned his jacket, and left, still holding his hand across his face. The little girl chased him for a few steps into the yard, and then came back.

"Haul some snow," said Fleur. She handed Lulu a bucket, and then spread her hand over the rounded slope of her stomach and stood in the doorway, absorbed. Then she moved again. Margaret had demanded that Eli come help Nector chop and haul a load of wood to sell. She drove along with them to make sure they got the best price. They were gathering money to pay the family land fees, due late spring. Because the others were gone, I did not mind stripping down, although I tried to hold a blanket up for modesty.

"We're all skinny this year," said Fleur, tugging at my shield. I tried holding it around me, made her pull the harder, till she jerked at me in annoyance and struggled to put me in the water. She ripped off my homemade underwear, threw my shift and knickers in a steaming iron cauldron. She also had a smaller kettle boiling, and a couple large tin kerosene cans of water that she poured into the washtub along with the snow. I stepped into the warmth.

"Don't sit down yet," said Lulu. I cowered in her gaze. She was a bossy little thing, an odd, vain, far too intelligent child. She dribbled warm water down my legs. The patent leather shoes she kept hooked to her belt swung lightly. I was hypnotized, calmed by their shine, for I gave myself up then, closed my eyes and decided not to question Fleur's habit of sudden tenderness. It was like that night she carried me to Fritzie's closet and lay me among the ledgers. I gave in. But I would not accept the cloth and brush they put into my hand. I had made a rule never to touch myself, to scratch, to rub a strained muscle, wash or cleanse. I could not break my vow, for all of Fleur's exasperation. I let them take my clothes out to the yard to air over a smudge fire of slow-burning sage and sweetgrass. Then Fleur washed me, but I warned myself not to experience any pleasure. I sat down in the water, felt its heat as a sharp danger, but then I forgot. The child soaped my back with a slick plant, and scrubbed away the agonizing itch of rough twine and harsh woolens. I gave her my hand. She washed each finger, then each toe. Fleur pared the overgrown nails with a knife. The girl rinsed away the sting of nettles, aggravation of hooked burrs. She dislodged the invisible strands of screwgrass that had woven into my skin. Fleur poured a pitcher of warm water over me and then began to shampoo my head and hair. It was so terrible, so pleasant, that I abandoned my Lord and all His rules and special requirements. I think I fell asleep, lost awareness, let the water course over me and let the hands on my hips, my throat, my back, my breasts, the cupped hands under my chin and around my feet, break me down.

There was silence between Fleur's instructions, as if she was still listening, in that odd way, absorbed. The lamp was lit. The dusk came heavily, and when I was clean and dried, I went to visit the outhouse. Fleur had thrown my nest of underclothes out in the woods once they boiled apart. She gave me floursacks to wear, luxuriously smooth. The habit was warm against my newly opened skin and the cold air rushed in through the pores of my hands and face. The wind was like an elixir that put me mindless and at peace. I felt no jealousy or zeal. I purified myself and then, very quietly, returned.

I saw the blood first, a small brilliant patch where she'd dropped the metal tub after emptying it in the yard. There was more leading into the house and inside. The lamp was shining on the table and Fleur was lying flat on the sleeping bed all wrapped in blankets, with Lulu unfrightened beside her.

"Listen," she said to me, her voice strong. "Go out to the lean-to where I keep my plants and bring back alder. Boil some for me."

"What's wrong?" I asked.

"Too soon," she answered. "Alder stops it."

So I left mother and daughter in the half-light and went into the tiny tacked-on room hung with wrapped leaves and roots, small packets of bark, as well as several packages of ground wheat, acorns, lake rice in tight birchbark containers. That was the food they had left for the winter, I know. In my haste I knocked the containers to the floor and they broke for mice. But I was shaking. And I could not remember the plant's configuration, even though its use was common enough for bleeding problems.

"What does it look like?" I cried.

She shouted, impatient. "You know! In the corner, tied in a brown cloth."

I heard the bed creak, her feet on the floor, the steps she took before she halted and went silent. I heard the bed again and knew that she did not dare move.

I swung the lantern high. Plant after plant! Some were shaped like a man's forked legs and some were rolled in balls. Some were wrapped tight in reeds and some were strewn about, careless, gathered from the woods or shore or the bottom of the lake. Bernadette had her remedies too. But they were all in bottles, labeled, mainly bought from a store. I put forth my hand, thinking, what can I do? Lord, tell me! I swept through the dry things and don't know what I seized.

She was fighting to breathe evenly, trying not to move the slightest of her muscles when I came back into the room. There was more blood, on the blankets this time, and on the floor where she had tried to rise.

"Do you have it?" she said.

I could only nod. Lulu was bundling on her coat.

"I'm going to Grandma's and bring them back," she said, her voice raised importantly. I dropped the dried plant in the pan of water and said nothing when the girl put her thin fancy shoes on and skipped outside, so pleased with herself, but determined, running very fast.

Fleur's eyes were closed. Her face was drained of color. I knew this look and I was fascinated, rapt, as at other death- and sickbeds. The glowing scarf was not more than one shade paler than her brow, and the earrings were hidden and dull. She said that I should fetch moss to stem the blood, fetch rags, scrape the root upwards, into the water, find a small leather packet and some other leaves. "This is too fast," she said, her voice rising a pitch.

I moved away from her, fumbled in the woodbox, down in corners, tipped the water over, scalding my own leg, and had to boil it again. I do not know why the Lord overtook my limbs and made them clumsy, but it must have been His terrible will. I never was like this during sickness before, not since Bernadette taught me. But I could not work my arms, my hands properly, my fingers. The only sound in the cabin was the bed, a rocking movement, the hold and release of Fleur's breath.

"When are they coming!" she muttered after some time had passed, and then, "Get over here!"

I moved to her, shaking, tripped on my own feet. She clutched my arms and dug in her fingers, the talons of a heavy bear. She spoke into my face, her eyes deep and ringed, and said no and kept saying no over and over again as the baby slid from her. Then she threw down my arm with all her strength and I flew across the room. I kept watching in the spill of light as she raised herself with vast effort and took the child from her own blood, then the knife from its sheath where it hung from the bedframe. She cut the cord and breathed into the child's mouth, rubbed its skin and changed its dead gray color. When it cried out she bound it tightly against her, into her shirt. I watched her breathe hard, gather strength, before she got up to her feet and staggered to the lean-to, the stove where she came back to scrape the root, to where she dripped water over the shavings with an awful patience, and added a crumbling powder of bees dried and crushed. She boiled the mixture, sat on the floor, held the child against her and drank. She cooled some of the medicine in her mouth and tried to give it to the baby. The lamp burned low and neither of us moved to fill it. I thought she might have died, propped against the wall, but then after some time had passed, she dragged herself upright along the boards. I sat still, stunned in prayer.

She reared over me, great and dark as a fixed tree.

Oh God who has seen fit to prove Thyself through the vessel of a woman, through me, Oh God who bound my wrists, who tripped me, Lord and Author of all Lies, hear Pauline.

I saw that she was dying, despite the medicines, despite all that I could do, all the prayers I had lifted. And that baby would go with her. The stillness lasted so long it became a threat and then a certainty. She would take me as well. I sat paralyzed. Fleur tightened one arm about the bundle in her shirt. She tossed the other arm high. I didn't see her though. I was dazed in the gold of the serpent's twirling eyes. Her face was hidden as if in a cowl. The room was so dark I could not see but only hear the whisper of the knife, at which I threw my legs apart. The blade stuck in the wood, and I was pinned there through layers of wool and cotton.

Then we were held in that night together.

The fire in the stove went out, the moon rode behind a cloud. The lamp recovered for a moment and I saw Fleur walk to the door, open it, step through. A swirling blackness lowered, lifted, and when I pulled away, the knife from between my thighs dropped. I followed her, the way I had in Argus, drawn against my judgment. She was barefoot, with no real coat. My clothes were newly washed and heavy. Yet I was cold. The ice on the crust of snow cut my ankles through my stockings, and the wind shook needles against my face. I thought I'd turn back but then the trees groaned and whined, almost covering the baby's cries, and my steps quickened to find if it would stay alive. I came up behind them, dogged their vague blue forms as they walked down the trail at the edge of the lake, a path that broadened when it swerved around the village to run due west.

I had been everywhere on the reservation, but never before on this road, which was strange because it was so wide and so furiously trodden that the snow was beaten to a rigid ice. I imitated Fleur when she pulled two pieces of bark off a tree, tied them around her feet with a strip of her skirt. From then on we gained a quiet rhythm, our legs tireless and strong. There was no weakness in either of us. No fear. The cold was gone. We skated on our bark shoes, floated the iced pathway along with other Indians. How odd that there were so many, and still hungry, too. The twigs were snapped along the way for something to chew, and all the moving water sipped from the streams.

We glided west, following the fall of night in a constant dusk. We passed dark and vast seas of moving buffalo and not one torn field, but only earth, as it was before. The grass was high and brown some places, sheltered from the snow. Farther on, the snow was drifted in long wings, or swept bare. There were no fences, no poles, no lines, no tracks. The road we walked was the only sign of humans, and also where it led, which I knew only when it appeared.

Those who starved, drank, and froze, those who died of

the cough, all of the people I'd blessed, washed, and wrapped, all were here. The road ended in a long plain of shallow snow. Across the waste, I saw the cold green fires of their town. We passed my mother and father walking. I hid my face. I wanted to pull on Fleur's shoulder, ask her to turn back now, but she crept toward the closest blaze and stood outside a circle of people. They were huddled, watching a game. Three men played it.

I knew them all.

Lily sagged, almost gaunt, his eyes sunken red and rimmed with black skin. Tor mouthed his chewed cigar, and Dutch James, poor Dutch! What there was of him. He clutched cards in three fingers of his only hand. Mournful and gray, they still seemed half frozen. Their hair stuck fast as if in icicles, their hands were raw and white. They did not notice us, but others in the watching circles, Indians, turned to stare at Fleur with shining narrow eyes. There was Jean Hat, his chest still lean and crushed from the cart. There was Many Women, dripping from the tub. And Lazarre, who gestured at her violently and tapped his burst heart.

In the heaven of the Chippewa there is gambling with spears of wood and rounded stones. There is gambling with deer knuckles, small brown bones, cards, dice, and human teeth. Snips of copper, bone buttons, iron rings and coins and dollar bills are piled around the players for stakes. Sometimes there are jars of whiskey, purer and more potent than the whiskey here.

They play for drunkenness, or sorrow, or loss of mind. They play for ease, they play for penitence, and sometimes for living souls.

Fleur walked through the crowd.

"Deal me in," she said.

The dog was still there, solid but somewhat leaner in this world. It sprang alertly onto Lily's lap, shivered in hate. The game was draw, Lily's favorite, with one-eyed jacks wild. They started easy, placed low bets in the first round and went on. Discarded. Fleur built up a serviceable hand. The men's smiles tightened at the edges and released. They knew, of course, that Fleur could bluff. Lily pointed to her, indicating the child hidden in her shawl.

The men seemed certain of themselves and fanned their cards in flourishes or shut them with fast efficient snaps. They made the same small faces they had around the stove in Argus. I stood watching, quiet as I'd watched in Argus, hard against the wall of folded arms, so intent that I ceased to breathe and turned invisible, clear like water, thin as glass, so that my presence was finally nothing more than a slight distortion of the air.

They showed. Fleur lost the first round.

She fell forward as though struck and her hair tumbled down around her arms. A woman appeared, from behind she was the size and weight of my mother. I heard the whispers, the low talk, of how in her eagerness to die this woman had left her child among the living. She slowly put her hands out and pulled the swaddled baby from Fleur, whose face went stupid and motionless, who sat frozen until Lily from his vest pulled out a curl of hair, black and full of lights, Lulu's hair. In his fist he also clutched a small patent leather shoe. I started. I almost called out. Impossible! The child had worn those shoes as she ran for help that very same evening. Lily dropped the hair, the small shoe, upon the table and there these objects gleamed, alive among the polished rounds of bone that the players now anted and raised.

Fleur came back to herself and played. She fanned through her cards, hunched and drawn as an old witch woman, lean as a half-dead wolf, and desperate. When final show came, she breathed out, slow. The dog did not dare move or whine. Dutch yawned.

"Two pairs," he said, "eights high."

Lily took forever to turn his hand. It was a good hand, a full house, high ranking with the king of clubs and hearts. And then Tor came up with three of a kind, including the jack of hearts. It was Fleur's hand now and she turned her cards over one by one, slow.

Four queens, and last, the one-eyed jack of spades.

She snatched the lock of hair into her shirt and raked the pot of bone buttons to herself with an endless and wearied sweep of her arms. That moment seemed to last so very long, for the men turned to me then, picked me out among the watchers. Their eyes followed me through dead air no matter how small I made myself. The old trick did not work this time. I was visible. They saw me, and it was clear from their eyes they knew my arms had fixed the beam in the cradle, back in Argus. I had sent them to this place.

I grabbed Fleur's sleeve. We flew, we ran, we grew sails of our shawls. We went back down the road and blew into the cold, still cabin. Outside, I heard Margaret's quick footfalls on the hardcrusted snow.

I would have flung the door open and rushed to the old woman, grabbed her arm, but I was once more pinned tight by the knife Fleur had thrust into my skirt. I put my hands out, but Margaret barged past, whirled to Fleur's side, then away. She stoked the fire to a roar and heated the strong medicine Fleur had prepared. And all the time she did this, she jabbered to me, finding the blood, the cold ashes, how it was my fault, my fault, and my most grievous fault. She put the cup to Fleur's lips and cleaned Fleur's face. When Fleur opened her eyes and lifted her head, gained sense enough to drink on her own, I finally pried loose the blade. I went to Fleur's side, prayed out loud.

"I must baptize this soul," I said, and reached for the tiny form. I intended to pour a teaspoon of water on its brow. But Fleur's arm swung out, cut me across the throat like a branch. I slumped to my knees, struggled to regain my air, and could only watch as Margaret wrapped the unsaved in a good cloth, then laid it in the fancy brown box that had held Lulu's shoes. This she handed to Eli when he arrived. He took it in his hands and weighed it uncertainly, as if he half believed that it was empty. Then he doubled over, pressed the cardboard to his chest, and went out. They say he tied the box with strands of his own hair, high in the old growth of oaks, out of reach of anything that moved on the ground below.

A mistake.

I've read its name in the pattern of wet black twigs. I've heard it crying to its father, the presence in the lake. There is so much to be done now, so many plans and too few hours. Before Eli came back that morning, without the box, I had found the door in spite of my dread at the journey. I told Margaret that I was leaving, that I would ask Father Damien to visit. I would find Bernadette and she would make a strengthening broth.

Margaret's answer was to spit on my shoe, and when I

bent over, in humility, to wipe, she spat on the crown of my veil, so that before I rose I had to admonish myself in Christ's instruction, turn my cheek to more blows. I put out my hands.

"Here too," I said, holding my palms steady. I was foolish. She had the knife in her hand she had used to scrape the healing root. It flared out the second time that night, would have pierced me with Christ's stigmata, had I not clapped my palms together in a sudden prayer and jumped out the door, lighting backward in the snow.

But my hands did not escape punishment.

I left Matchimanito, then walked the trail down to the convent, where I arrived in time to lose myself in God's tasks. That morning, shattering ice from the buckets in the kitchen, I scraped my hand raw. But I continued to smash my fist into the water until the water told the story, turned faintly bloody, and someone, Superior I think it was, appeared at my side and held my fingers still in hers. She led me from the stove, dabbed my hand clean, wrapped it in a cloth.

"Go back to sleep," she said. "Even a Saint must rest."

CHAPTER SEVEN

Winter 1918–Spring 1919
Pauguk Beboon
Skeleton Winter

—

NANAPUSH

I went out for a stick of wood for Margaret's fire, and instead found you at the door, too dazed with frozen sleep to pound or call. I brought you in and laid you down. I don't know what you recall, my girl, but the sight is captured in my memory. Your stiffened fingers sifted the air. Your feet thumped on the table, blocks in those shoes of thin reflecting leather. Your lips parted and you spoke just enough to tell us there was something wrong at home, and then you started shaking so hard your teeth clacked, furious and fast as a bone rattle. Margaret warmed blankets on the stove to heat you, tore off your clothing, wrapped you naked in three hot layers of flannel. It was a night of deep cold, a sharp snow driving like fine dust, confusing any trail and obscuring the landmarks. You had twice lost your way and on top of that, vain girl, you wore your fancy shoes once you did not have to answer to your mother.

"Damn Eli for buying them!" Margaret yelled when she plucked off the pretty shoes. She was so mad she threw open the stove door and stuffed them into the fire. But soon they began to melt and stink, so she snatched them from the flames with a meatfork and threw them smoking into the snow.

Margaret ordered me to sit on the bed, and I obeyed her. She laid you in my lap and piled clothes on until I feared you'd smother, but you still shivered so hard you rippled from one end to the other and could not be stilled. Margaret drew the covers away from your poor feet and put one on either side of my chest, tucked into the hollows beneath my arms. I hunched over in shock at their ice-hardness. Then I absorbed the cold into myself.

"Hold on to her," said Margaret, layering herself in shawls, "no matter how hard she fights."

She put water within my reach, two cups, a bit of bread, and a spoon of grease. Then she headed for Matchimanito, left me to thaw my foolish, suffering granddaughter.

I'm sure you've forgotten what happened next, for if you remembered, you would not wear such shoes as you have on at this moment—those heels, like tiny knives, and your toes sticking through! You'd wear footwrappings made of rabbit fur for protection, and no fine stockings either. But I suppose you don't recall how it was when the blood rushed back into those feet. It is thanks to me that they still grow on the ends of two legs that cut a fast jig at French fiddle dances. You howled like a wildcat. You cursed me in surprising words. You flung off your blankets, thrashed and fought my hands as though you were drowning. But I know certain cure songs, words that throw the sick one into a dream and cause a low dusk to fall across the mind.

Many times in my life, as my children were born, I wondered what it was like to be a woman, able to invent a human from the extra materials of her own body. In the terrible times, the evils I do not speak of, when the earth swallowed back all it had given me to love, I gave birth in loss. I was like a woman in my suffering, but my children were all delivered into death. It was contrary, backward, but now I had a chance to put things into a proper order.

Eventually, my songs overcame the painful burning and you were suspended, eyes open, looking into mine. Once I had you I did not dare break the string between us and kept on moving my lips, holding you motionless with talking, just as at this moment. For the first time in my life, it was my duty as well as pleasure to hold forth all night and long into the next morning.

My tongue grew thick in my mouth when I'd sipped all the water. My throat clutched and my eyes itched for sleep. I did not stop. I talked on and on until you lost yourself inside the flow of it, until you entered the swell and ebb and did not sink but were sustained. I talked beyond sense— by morning the sounds I made were stupid mumbles without meaning or connection. But you were lulled by the roll of my voice.

Later that day, Father Damien heard of our troubles and brought some butter which I spread on your frostbitten cheeks. He also brought along another something I did not want, the off-reservation doctor whom I could not trust. He was a busy man, especially since the returning hero Pukwan brought influenza, from the east, within the folds of his uniform. This doctor was known to refuse Indians to our face, but did not dare say no to a priest. The man was bearded, huge, clumsy-looking like a weak-sighted bear, but he handled your feet as if they were delicate, the eggs of a thrush. He weighed them in his fingers and stared, tested them gently all over, then felt through his case for a bottle. It was laudanum, I'd seen it before, and I'd read of it in my papers. He gave some to you and waited until your eyes closed before he spoke. Yes! Yes I know! Your sleep was pretense. Even then, I knew you listened.

"All of one froze," he said. "Half the other. I'll take her to my office, I have a motorcar."

He packed the bottle into his bag and put on his coat.

"She stays here," I answered.

"She'll die of the festering." He tried to muscle past, but I would not allow it.

"Reason with the idiot," he commanded poor Damien, who was caught in the web of his meddling. Father tried talking to me earnestly, face to face, and did his best to no effect. Tears started in his eyes and his shoulders sagged, but I would not budge. We all knew what was unsaid, but only I knew you. You were no quiet child, no pensive thing who could survive without running. You were a butterfly, a flash of wit and fire, a blur of movement who could not keep still. Saving you the doctor's way would kill you, which did not mean I was completely confident in my ability to save you, either.

The doctor slammed out and stamped down the path. I heard his automobile engine catch, and I fought back the urge to rush after him. Then you opened your eyes, addled by the doctor's syrup, and gave me a flushed, secret look. When you're married and have your children, you will know this: We don't have as much to do with our young as we think. They do not come from us. They just appear, as if they broke through a net of vines. Once they live in our lives and speak our language, they slowly seem to become like us. But Lulu, sinking past my sight then, you were not enough like me yet to tell me where you were going or how long you would stay.

For days and days after I nursed you, and although I was still weak myself, I was a good doctor. I bathed those feet in water and pickling salt, fanned them with purifying smoke. I had to keep you with me although your mother wanted you back at Matchimanito, pleaded for you, would not be convinced you were living. When I sent a lock of hair with Margaret, your grandma reported that Fleur screamed at the sight and tore it from her hand, demanding the rest of you. She would only be comforted by your presence, that was clear. So on the first warm day I brought you to her on a small toboggan, the way I had once transported Fleur herself, the first winter of her troubles.

I packed all that I needed, all that was important to me, including the three-legged kettle my wives had used. I would stay at Matchimanito now until spring thaw, and planned to use the time convincing Margaret she needed me more than the sorry house she once shared with Kashpaw. As if Margaret knew my intentions, she put me off at once. She met you and me on the path and instructed me where I should set up my bedding. Not in her corner.

"As you'll see," she said, "we'll have to keep our senses sharpened."

I protested. "That's exactly what your touches do to mine . . ."

"Hush up."

Fleur leaned against the house, and the sight of her shut my mouth. She was wasted, her bones sharp and raw, smudged in the face with dirt and ragged in her hair and clothes, wild as the day I wrestled her as Pukwan looked on in fear.

A sound tore from her, harsh and strange. She lurched through the snow, hair dragging from the streaked scarf, hands stretching for her daughter. Delighted, you opened your mouth wide and laughed at the game. Your mother had played this with you before, curled her fingers in claws, pretended to be a dangerous rugaroo.

But Fleur was dangerous. We lose our children in different ways. They turn their faces to the white towns, like Nector as he grew, or they become so full of what they see in the mirror there is no reasoning with them anymore, like you. Worst of all is the true loss, unbearable, and yet it must be borne. Fleur heard her vanished child in every breath of wind, every tick of dried leaves, every scratch of blowing snow. One sleeting night before anyone could stop her, she took but one thing, vanished out the door. Eli followed her into the woods and whispered to us, later, that she had propped and wedged the black umbrella high in the tree, sheltering the box strung with ribbons and hair.

But after that, because of your demands, your mother roused herself. She woke one morning, rose early, and sat down with me, her face bright.

"Uncle," she smiled, holding my hand, "today we'll eat fresh venison."

She told Eli of the path that had appeared in her sleep, a complicated trail through the woods, where the deer tracks began. He listened to her, even repeated her directions to make certain that he had them memorized. Then, in great excitement, he took his gun, a handful of dried rosehips, and went out. All that day we fasted easily, anticipating his return. But he came back empty-handed. The snow where she sent him was smooth and bare. There was no sign of so much as a rabbit or a squirrel.

"We'll chew twigs tonight," Fleur said. Her voice was light but her face was set, and nothing more escaped her lips.

The next day just after dawn she went down to the shores of Matchimanito and crossed the ice, chopped a hole in it, and let down a line for fish. Eli followed and had to argue with her, then fight with her, then drag her back across the ice when her legs weakened and would not bear even the slight weight of her, so thin. He went back and watched the line she set, nearly froze his hand to it in his anxiousness, but caught nothing but a weak runt perch.

The fish was cooked without a word, eaten to the last fin. That evening, light snow began and Fleur stalked to the door, turned away several times, sat in the deep yellow light of the translucent windows, and sang words I hadn't heard before, chilling and cold as the dead, restless and sharp as the wind of the month when the trees crack.

"Come to sleep," I told her.

Fleur didn't hear me. She was listening through the walls, through the air and snow, down into the earth which was no shelter for us now. She sat there all night with her hands folded in her lap, but in the end it was not Fleur's dreams, my skill, Eli's desperate searches, or Margaret's preserves that saved us. It was the government commodities sent from Hoopdance in six wagons.

The day the rations arrived, we knew that one of us would have to go into town and register for food with the Agent, yet nobody moved. We let our weakness overcome us. Every so often a voice would call out, from a corner, that it was time to get ready now, to go, but then no one would move and another long quiet would fall.

We might have laid there like fools and starved had it not been for Margaret. She finally got bored with suffering and berated us as she rose and put on her wrappings.

"This never would have happened at the Kashpaw place," she said. "People stick together there."

She slammed the door, went down the hill, and came back with Father Damien, who'd signed a paper for us. In his pack he had a slab of bacon, a can of lard, a sack of flour, and a twist of baking powder. Margaret had rice and a pound of green coffee beans. Unbelievably, her pockets bulged with turnips. Fleur met her at the end of the trail, grabbed and emptied the pockets, took the turnips from her, turned them over in her hands. She walked in the door and carried them to the stove. I saw them, round and dark gold. They looked like treasures.

My head was light and my breath came fast. I hardly seemed to touch ground when I walked toward the priest and shook his hand. I wanted to eat with him, then talk, to hear news of everything happening in town. But Father Damien had other surprises.

"Sit down," he said, "sit down all together."

Then he pulled out the annual fee lists and foreclosure notices sent by the Agent and showed us how most families, at the end of this long winter, were behind in what they owed, how some had lost their allotments. We traced the list until we found the names we sought—Pillager, Kash-paw, Nanapush. All were there, figures and numbers, and all impossible. We stared without feeling at the amounts due before summer.

We watched as Damien unfolded and smoothed the map flat upon the table. In the dizzy smell of coffee roasting, of bannock cooking, we examined the lines and circles of the homesteads paid up—Morrissey, Pukwan, Hat, Lazarres everywhere. They were colored green. The lands that were gone out of the tribe—to deaths with no heirs, to sales, to the lumber company—were painted a pale and rotten pink. Those in question, a sharper yellow. At the center of a bright square was Matchimanito, a small blue triangle I could cover with my hand.

The bread was passed around and all of us tried hard not to lose control, to wolf each crumb into ourselves with snarls, to cry out at the goodness of it. We spread the lard on each piece, everyone concentrated on each slow bite, and there was no sound but chewing. Although Father Damien would not join us in eating, he didn't seem to mind the lack of conversation. His troubled eyes were trained on the map.

Eventually, our attentions focused too.

With her fingernail, Margaret traced the print she could not read, polished first the small yellow Kashpaw square, then tapped the doubled green square of Morrisseys, and gestured at Fleur and Eli to compare.

"They're taking it over."

It was like her to notice only the enemies that she could fight, those that shared her blood however faintly. My concern was the lapping pink, the color of the skin of lumberjacks and bankers, the land we would never walk or hunt, from which our children would be barred.

Eli made an angry sound and bit his lip, but Fleur laid her hand on my shoulder and let the silence gather around her before she spoke with contempt for the map, for those who drew it, for the money required, even for the priest. She said the paper had no bearing or sense, as no one would be reckless enough to try collecting for land where Pillagers were buried.

Margaret muttered as she turned away from her daughter-in-law. "She's living in the old days when people had respect."

I could not agree with Fleur either, for already I had seen too many changes. Dollar bills cause the memory to vanish, and even fear can be cushioned by the application of government cash. I closed my eyes against Fleur's anger and I saw this: leaves covering the place where I buried Pillagers, mosses softening the boards of their grave houses, once so gently weeded and tended by Fleur. I saw the clan markers she had oiled with the sweat of her hands, blown over by wind, curiosities now, a white child's toys.

"As you know, I was taught by the Jesuits," I said to Damien. "I know about law. I know that 'trust' means they can't tax our parcels."

The young priest's neck had thinned, his cheeks hollowed. To shield himself from the cold he had tried to grow a beard but it was too sparse for warmth. He shook his head now, unwilling to deliver what he had to tell.

I pointed to his chin, tried to force him to smile. "That pelt would fetch no more than a nickel from the trader."

Nector jumped in and said what poor Damien found difficult.

"If we don't pay they'll auction us off!"

Damien nodded, went on, ignoring Margaret's shocked poke at her knowledgeable son. "Edgar Pukwan Jr. and the Agent control the choosing of the board who will decide who may bid on what foreclosed parcels, and where."

"They know better," Fleur said with confidence that seemed pitiful and false to me, though I had never before pitied Pillagers. "They won't dare throw us off the shores of this lake," she promised.

Father Damien had already heard otherwise. "There's some who want to build a fishing lodge," he said in a gentle voice. "They're willing to trade for an allotment someplace else."

Fleur refused to hear this, but I could not ignore it and digested this new betrayal in silence. My thoughts were everywhere, a swarm of gnats, a flock of arguments. Pillager land was not ordinary land to buy and sell. When that family came here, driven from the east, Misshepeshu had appeared because of the Old Man's connection. But the water thing was not a dog to follow at our heels.

"We will have to raise the money," I said, but even I could hear the hopeless question in my voice.

Margaret, however, seemed ready for this moment. She had been in deep thought at the stove, piercing the turnips as they boiled. She banged her fork on the burner. All of our attention clung to her and she pursed her lips in satisfaction at the plan that was growing in her mind. She paused a moment to marvel, within herself, at the splendor and timing of her information. Fleur was the first to thump her foot on the floor and mutter, "Well?"

Margaret's modest smile was a small neat bow that she would not untie. She enjoyed our puzzled helplessness too long, however, for it was the priest who finally filled us in on the Pinkham's dealer, who was buying the bark of certain wild shrubs.

"Mishkeegamin," Margaret explained hurriedly, to throw him off.

The tonic dealer came to town each week with an empty wagon for cranberry bark, and from that day we were ready for him every time, although it meant we stripped every bush around Matchimanito, and when that was done ranged still farther into the outskirts of the woods. We came back every night with great bundles of sticks, tongues rancid from the watery berries even the birds had left, and we sat down together to peel. By the end of the week the floor was deep to the calves with the curling strings of bark. The thin pungent odor stuck to us, lodged in our clothes, and would be with us forever as the odor of both salvation and betrayal, for I was never able to walk in the woods again, to break a stick of cranberry without remembering the outcome of the toil that split the skin on our fingers. The bark also dulled us with lack of sleep, for every turn, every shift, every quiet sneaking to the pail in the lean-to at night, caused the lake of drying peels on the floor to rustle like waves, so that from then on that winter there was never silence, but a constant shuffling and scratching, a money sound that dragged around us, an irritation.

Eli walked back to town when the turnips were eaten, brought home the rest of the supplies that were due us, and so the back of the famine broke. But in this there was something lost.

Fleur had not saved us with her dream, and it now seemed

what was happening was so ordinary that it fell beyond her abilities. She had failed too many times, both to rescue us and save her youngest child, who now slept in the branches of bitter oaks. Her dreams lied, her vision was obscured, her helper slept deep in the lake, and all her Argus money was long spent. Though she traveled through the bush with gunnysacks and her skinning knife, though she worked past her strength, tireless, and the rough shreds piled to our ankles and spilled across the floor, Fleur was a different person than the young woman I had known. She was hesitant in speaking, false in her gestures, anxious to cover her fear.

I pressed charcoal into her hand one day. "Go down to the shore," I told her. "Make your face black and cry out until your helpers listen."

But she would not. "I'm tired, old Uncle." The sound of her complaint was bright and hollow. She crept toward the bed and when she thought I was not looking, she eased herself under the blankets and lay with her face to the wall. I smoked a pipe, and I thought of what I'd say to her if only she would listen.

Power dies, power goes under and gutters out, ungraspable. It is momentary, quick of flight and liable to deceive. As soon as you rely on the possession it is gone. Forget that it ever existed, and it returns. I never made the mistake of thinking that I owned my own strength, that was my secret. And so I never was alone in my failures. I was never to blame entirely when all was lost, when my desperate cures had no effect on the suffering of those I loved. For who can blame a man waiting, the doors open, the windows open, food offered, arms stretched wide? Who can blame him if the visitor does not arrive?

I told this to Fleur that same day. I made her sit down and listen, just the way you are sitting now. Your mother always showed the proper respect to me. Even when I bored her, she made a good effort at pretending some interest. She never tapped her fingers on her uncovered knees, shuffled and twisted and made faces out the window like you. Even on that afternoon, when I told her things she could not hear, there was no impatience in her manner and she thanked me for my advice. But in her bearing, as she rose and walked away from me, I saw the barrier of her obstinate pride had kept my words safely beyond belief. In her mind she was huge, she was endless. There was no room for the failures of anyone else. At the same time, she was the funnel of our history. As the lone survivor of the Pillagers, she staggered now beneath the burden of a life she was failing to deserve.

"You are my daughter," I called after her. "Your child has my name on a church paper. Listen to me."

She turned to me and managed to put a mask of patience upon her face. Fleur lifted her hands up to her temples, beside her slanting eyes, and smoothed back her hair from the planes of her cheeks.

"You will not be to blame if the land is lost," I told her, "or if the oaks and the pines fall, the lake dries, and the lake man does not return. You could not have saved the child that came so early."

This last, however, she could not bear and whirled away from me. She ran, her hands formed into muffs around her ears.

As the last weeks of winter dragged out, more news came to us, gossip of things that happened to our enemies.

First, we heard that Pauline had sworn to take her vows. Then that Sophie and Clarence Morrissey both married Lazarres. Some said those were forbidden partners, cousins in their own clan, but others maintained we were so mixed in with French now it didn't matter. They went to be married at a distant church in Canada, where the fact that they were related was not mentioned or known. One after the other, returning to the reservation, they walked into the Morrissey house. First Clarence told Bernadette what he had done and displayed his bride, shy and sullen. Bernadette slumped to the floor in shock. So she was sitting there already when Sophie entered with her Lazarre, Izear, who already had six children by a wife many thought he'd killed.

Bernadette jumped up. She kicked Clarence in the knee and slapped Sophie until her cheeks were red, but her children moved their spouses in right past her yells. Her new grandchildren took immediate charge of the house. They put their feet through the wicker chair seats, devoured the soup in the kettle before it had boiled, poured sugar straight from the sack into their mouths. But it was not until she went to the cellar the next morning and found every pickle jar empty, that Bernadette packed to leave. She wrapped up the baby she called Marie, and grabbed Philomena's arm. The rest happened quickly. Part and parcel, she moved to town. In a week, with her cleanliness, her methodical handwriting, and her way with sums, she had found a way to save her land. In spite of the first consumptive signs in her lungs, Bernadette kept house for the Agent, reorganized his property records, and mailed debt announcements to every Indian in arrears.

Napoleon, deserted by his sister and surrounded by a

horde of tormenting relatives, began to drink steadily as if to block them from his view. People get the grandchildren they deserve: I got you. Napoleon, the relatives of this husband you think you want. So take a lesson from what an old man knows and think about this Morrissey twice! Let me tell you how that pack of dogs existed.

One day, in spite of the head shaving and the death of Lazarre, in spite of Sophie keeling over outside Fleur's cabin, I took Nector with me and together we set foot on Morrissey land. Who would ever think such a thing would happen? And yet we old-time Indians were like this, long-thinking but in the last, forgiving, as we must live close together, as one people, share what we have in common, take what we're owed, for instance Napoleon's last cow.

He was getting ready to butcher the poor caved-in beast when I walked into the yard. Sophie, a jacket held around the swollen shape of the first child of many she would bear, stood outside the door. Her face was puffy, hair in ragged knots, teeth browning in streaks from the last bits of candy on the reservation. Napoleon sharpened a knife on a jutting stone, next to a ring in the ground to which the cow was tethered. His unwanted relative, Izear, crouched to one side with a washtub and another knife. Clarence was loading the gun that he would use.

He pretended not to notice us, but his shoulders adjusted, and it seemed to me he swallowed hard, from reflex. He poised the gun, his billed cap low across his eyes. He took aim and the cow swayed in a trance. It was Izear Lazarre who spoke first.

"Stand back you beggars, we'll throw you the guts."

Nector blushed, then found his tongue and glared at Clarence, rubbed his neck and spoke to me in a loud and offhand voice.

"Uncle, when you catch a rabbit, you leave your mark."

"Remember how we spared the life of that one?" I asked my nephew. "Sometimes you let a rabbit live until you need him."

"What rabbit?" Izear wanted to know.

Clarence lowered the gun, motionlessly alert. Then I knew that the Morrissey had not told his shame, which gave me advantage.

"It happened this way..." I began, turning to include Sophie, and Napoleon, who bent down at an angle, drunk, straw caught around his ears.

"What are you after?" Clarence demanded.

"You owe half the carcass, at least," I said.

"A quarter," said Clarence, tense. "We need the rest."

Izear's six ferrets burst half-dressed from the house and surrounded the cow, climbing its back, pulling its udders, counting its knobs and ribs, until it shuddered. The poor thing sagged under their attack until its knees buckled, its head thumped to earth. When Clarence had beaten them off, we saw the cow lay huddled on folded legs, hips jutting, stone dead.

Sophie came out, herded her young ones back into the house with the promise of molasses. I looked around while Clarence butchered my share, which shrank beneath his knife. Already, mark this, the place had changed to what it is now. The windows were broken out with planks and dirty oiled paper hung in their place. Garbage, the snapped bones of muskrats, crushed cans and splinters of crates were littered in the crusted snow. Even the green paint Bernadette had set on the outside boards was scorched in places, scraped or marred. No smoke came from the chimney, but from inside could be heard the clank of pots and the shrieks and accusations of feeding children.

This picture was the start of what happened to the Morrisseys. They lost status as the years went on, as the bitterness between our families deepened. The will to plant and harvest deserted them. They ceased to keep their books and breed their stock in their rush to breed with each other. Granddaughter, if you join this clan, I predict the union will not last.

Listen to experience and marry wisely. I always did.

In late winter, the fish in the lake swarmed to the surface and we netted them through holes in the ice. Once we started eating food we caught for ourselves, my bad dreams stopped. The nights were peaceful and black. In the air the smell of water, earth softening beneath the snow, swelled and blew. The length of daylight expanded, slowly at first, then unmistakably. We ate in the morning, at midday, after sundown. After a month of food I began to look at Margaret as I had before the deprivations.

"Darling sweetheart," I said one afternoon, a warm day just before the ice broke on the lake.

She was making a powder of fish, something else to sell in town. She stirred the pieces in a cauldron over fire, seared, dried the flesh, broke it until it sifted fine. The strings from the black coal bonnet fluttered in the heat. The hardships of the winter had made her angular, yet she held herself straight.

"It has been long enough," she announced.

I went to her. You were fetching bark with Eli and your mother, Nector too. You think I'm going to stop at this point, but I'll go on. You have no one to prepare you for a husband, no sisters and no aunts, and Margaret would never admit to any weakness. So I'm going to tell you something about married people. Possibly, you know already, but dear girl, pretend for my sake that you don't?

The house was empty and your grandmother and I went inside, pulled the string through the latch, and lay down together in the smoky blankets of the bed. I lifted Margaret's bonnet and touched her strange hair. It glowed, grown out pure white and shaggy as an ermine that turns colorless as snow. I drew near and touched the rest of her and soon we were close together.

Margaret was bold, she was inventive, and in fact made such pleasing accommodations that I knew without a doubt these movements were practiced, refined. I was delighted in her experience. I wanted to last forever, tried not to respond. But she was so adept that I was a boy in her hand, forceful and warm as a chinook. I've seen ducks fly backward when the wind is blowing. I did too. And I don't know what else, for she had the best of me. Sometime before the others returned, I was amazed to see the light long in the bare trees, the shadows stretching blue.

"We have to build a little house out here this summer," I said. "We don't have time to waste. We need a place that's only for us."

"You only talk old," she said. "We'll get enough together for the fees on our own land, yours and mine. Then we'll decide which place suits us."

She was so certain, and, I thought at the time, so bad at money figures, that she didn't know we'd only just manage the payment on Matchimanito if we continued to work as hard as possible. She turned away, back to her fire and her work, banged the spoon on the cauldron later and cried, joking me, "I wouldn't live in a fall-down old bachelor's lean-to!"

We heard the sounds of your returning, and in our haste to smooth our dress and appear dignified, we had no time to finish our conversation.

It didn't matter anyway. My old home and fragment of land had stood empty and foreclosed upon for less than a month when a pack of Lazarres moved in and hung their mission clothes out the windows. It seemed they were every-place now, multiplying and dividing, taking up the cracks and crevices between the clans, the gaps that illness had left. No house stayed empty, no land unclaimed. There was always a Lazarre, a young and ready one to fill it, with a new wife or husband, a child, and all of them grown stout and greasy from the meat supplies that they had pilfered from their neighbors and the lard from the Agent's store-house.

It was hard for me to see this happen.

"We Indians are like a forest," I had said once to Damien. "The trees left standing get more sun, grow thick."

But now I spoke differently. A crippling poison had fol-lowed on the tail end of disease.

One day the priest walked the long way around to visit us, as the lake ice was unreliable. We arranged ourselves on rocks in the strengthening light, and remembered the winter's ravages. Just that spring, coming home from a sickhouse early one morning, the priest had stumbled across a child dressed in nothing but snow, bedded in the frozen leaves, skin black as charred wood. The house to which this tiny girl belonged was sleeping with the windows open and the doors locked. Everyone inside was blind drunk and raved, when they awakened, with pity for themselves, their loss, one less.

This was the poison, the affliction.

"You must step forward," said Damien. "Worse things are going to happen."

"I am old wood and I burn easily," I said. "My anger would scorch those around me."

"That is why you should get yourself into a leadership position," he said. "You must gain the Agent's ear, help make these decisions, find ways to prohibit whiskey traders from roosting on the reservation boundary."

Though young, his face had wrinkled into fine folds around the eyes and mouth. His brown hair had been cut too short to show a curl, and it was fine, almost bald in the front. Up close he looked strange, like an aged child. His ideas were good, no doubt. But I saw the snare right then, the invisible loop hidden in the priest's well-meaning words. Unlike the Pukwans, who were government Indians, I saw the deadfall beneath my feet before I stepped. I would avoid the job. I knew what was attached.

"Wires," I said, "tied to the hands and the arms."

Father Damien looked at me closely, with slow apprehension. He started in again with more reasons, more persuasions. He used everything I'd showed him about talking, did not let me get a word in, let no thought sink into my brain. I had taught him well.

"You write the letter then," I said, giving up. "Recommend me. Or however it is done."

And so he did, but from Bernadette, new secretary to the Agent of the government, there was no answer at that time.

Your feet had toughened in new moccasins, Lulu, and now you never took a quiet step but drummed from the woods to your mother's silence, bringing stones and bits of snow. You held Fleur's dress, fed her strips of meat from a bowl, combed her hair with your short fingers. She kept you close, which was understandable, but then she kept you closer. You could not wander from her sight even for a moment. If you walked across the inside of the cabin, she'd follow, or if you rounded the stove, hid for an instant behind the table, she caught you and dragged you into the open. She would not let you play in the lean-to, where you kept the wooden dolls I had whittled, and the clothing you made out of scraps and leaves. Outside, you could not go around the corner of the house for she'd pull you back, hold you tight and kiss your face until you struggled in her arms.

"I'll watch her down by the lake," Margaret said to Fleur. "You rest." I tried also. But Fleur trusted no one to care for you in the world that seemed so dangerous to her now. She jumped at the crack of a stick, any small sound, and whirled suddenly, only to confront a breath of wind. Eli did not complain loudly, although you slept between them every night, kicked and turned, poked at him before dawn so that he moped all day for lack of good sleep.

Margaret was not one to keep silent, however, and urged your freedom. "Lulu is well now, her feet have healed. Let her run!"

But if you ran, Fleur accompanied you, step for step in

the softening snow. I am a man, but for years I had known how it was to lose a child of my blood. Now I also knew the uncertainties of facing the world without land to call home. I recognized the signs in Fleur, but Margaret did not, for she had not lost one child in all her twelve, unheard-of luck, and she was confident that the great brown sacks of gathered bark, the tin box of money we'd collected, would save the Pillager allotments and us all, Kashpaws too. She had no way to understand Fleur's behavior. It was my idea that a cure, an easing, must take place, and my intention to go ask for help from Moses Pillager.

Although the ice along the shore was weak and rotten, I made my way out to his island. The sun had shone now for days on those rocks and the path stank sharply of cats. The wilder ones flung themselves across my trail like scarves; the ones that Moses petted and indulged twined in and out of my steps. They spread themselves on warm patches of ground, or crouched in branches. The air was quiet. Birds shunned the place, and the nets that flowed and billowed in the tree branches were empty. The path to the hut was well marked, and Moses stood outside the door, which was a great flap of hide fastened over the rocky entrance.

He was pleased to see me, amazed to have a guest. He smiled and made a low humming sound of contentment at my gift of tobacco. We drank a soup of fish powder and potatoes. Against the cold, Moses wore a garment made of tanned furs, all colors and markings, stripes and spots. It rippled and fluffed when he moved, and in the dry air, when cats brushed and rubbed against it, sparks crackled between the hairs.

I said to Moses that I was visiting him as Jeesekeewinini. I gave him some braids of sweetgrass that Margaret had gathered and dried. I gave him a knife and a bag of fish heads for his cats.

His face spoke gladness. Up high, in the corner of the rafters where the cats could not reach, Moses kept his drum. He uncovered it, put some of my offering in its tobacco box, and returned to sit with me. Then we both became serious, smoked the pipe. I described Fleur's illness, the cure I proposed, and told Moses when I needed him to appear.

Two days after, before a night with no moon, he walked across the ice bearing two of his drums. One was no more than a tin pail, across which a rawhide was stretched and bound. The other, fancier one was strapped to his back. This instrument was never allowed to touch the ground, and was decorated with long ribbons, with beaded skirt and tabs. It was painted for the directions, with a clawed spirit figure on one side.

There are two plants. One is yarrow and the other I will not name. These are the sources of my medicine, and I used them for the second time on Fleur, the third time on a Pillager. Only because of Pauline, I did not complete the job.

I mixed and crushed the ingredients. The paste must be rubbed on the hands a certain way, then up to the elbows, with exact words said. When I first dreamed the method of doing this, I got rude laughter. I got jokes about little boys playing with fire. But the person who visited my dream told me what plants to spread so that I could plunge my arms into a boiling stew kettle, pull meat from the bottom, or reach into the body itself and remove, as I did so long ago with Moses, the name that burned, the sickness.

Moses cut willows and shaped them into a frame for my tent of blankets and skins. I put together my own drum from Margaret's kettle, covered and filled it partway with water so that it would make a sound to attract trouble and then drown it inside. We worked quickly. Not long, and we had everything prepared the proper way. Then who should enter, walking tentative and slow, but the nun who could sniff out pagans because they once had been her relatives.

We waited for her to read the air around us and leave. But instead she sensed our lack of welcome and stayed, so that when I told Fleur to enter the tent, to breathe leaves I threw in the fire to make it smoke, she was at first distracted. Fleur laughed to see the novice nun crouched down in the corner, staring hungrily, closing her eyes to mutter prayers, occasionally erecting a protective cross in air. It is not our way to banish any guest. Margaret shushed Fleur, said that Pauline was a harmless, half-mad thing. Fleur shrugged, pretended to accept this, but I was worried, for the still look in Pauline's eyes made me wonder, so like a scavenger, a bird that lands only for its purpose.

I saw those eyes on Fleur.

The only light in the tent filtered from the hole above the fire. I built the blaze hot, hoping that the heat would penetrate gray wool, torment Pauline, drive her through the flap. Her brow gleamed, her white soap cheeks shone, her veils wetted and dragged around her shoulders. I fanned the coals until her smile stretched and pained. The water on the fire boiled, steam rose before me, and Moses began to sing. That is when I put my hands through the stirring cloud, into the swirl, and brought up a bit of choice meat. Fleur ate this very quietly, chewing slowly, taking strength.

The singing had affected her, driven away all humor, all notice of Pauline or anyone. And now, as she drank the brew from Margaret's bowl, two hard anxious lines carved deeply at each corner of her mouth.

Pauline crawled forward.

"I was sent," she blurted. Her face was a flat crude picture, a piece of paper with two round black holes cut for the eyes.

Margaret reached with a knot of wood and nudged at Pauline's chest, tried to prod her through the tentflaps without disturbing the curing airs around the drum and around Fleur. But Pauline batted the stick away.

"I'm sent to prove Christ's ways," she said.

Fleur's eyes closed, she leaned into the folded robes behind her. Her breath was shallow and her attention was directed within, so she did not witness Pauline's dreadful proof. We moved away from the fire and gave Pauline her wish. She prayed loudly in Catholic Latin, then plunged her hands, unprepared by the crushed roots and marrows of plants, into the boiling water. She lowered them farther, and kept them there. Her eyes rolled back into her skull and the skin around her cheeks stretched so tight and thin it nearly split. If she opened her mouth, I thought, pure steam might blast into the air. Moments passed. Then she shrieked, jumped. She clawed straight through the flimsy tent walls, scattering the willow poles, collapsing the blankets and skins around us all. Then she ran, by the light of her scalded arms, and followed the dark path back to town.

In the end, I do not know if it was the cure or the money that helped your mother. The deadline went by, but finally there came a day we put every cent in the house together, all we'd gathered in pay for Eli's tanned muskrat, beaver, otter hides, for Fleur's quill boxes, rabbitskin blankets, dried fish. We smoothed and stacked the dollars from the tin box, paid by Pinkham's remedies for gunnysacks of bark. I added money I had received for an old-time beaded bandolier, and Margaret drew from a moccasin twenty dollars in ancient nickels. Nector added bounties he'd collected on small animals. When it was all together, piled on the table, Margaret sat and counted the hoard. Father Damien came by and counted the money too, added the final quarter from his own pocket. Scooped together in a pouch, the fee payment made a thick and satisfying thump on the table. There was enough, just exactly as Margaret had predicted, for the holding money on both Pillager and Kashpaw land. No less, no more.

Perhaps, if your mother had herself taken the money in to the Agent, you would still be living on the shores of Matchimanito. But she was newly cheerful, trusting, drained from the work. Eli was trapping, my hip was lamed, and Nector was eager to take on responsibility.

And after, once he came back with the word, we were so glad and relieved that no one thought to ask for a receipt, no one noticed how often Nector took long trips hunting, or stayed in town, or with his mother on their land. I was the only one who felt hurt by how often Margaret left us. She spent days cleaning out her empty cellar, hours upon hours smoothing mudded mortar into the walls of the house built by Kashpaw. She had to work on me, rub me too, before I would join her. She was tough as the bristles on a brush, and I finally wore down. Without her I was despondent and I lived in the past, in former times, lost times when game was plenty, companions sharp with humor, times when it would have taken four days to walk the length of this reservation.

CHAPTER EIGHT

Spring 1919
Baubaukunaetae-geezis
Patches of Earth Sun

—

P A U L I N E

Christ was weak, I saw now, a tame newcomer in this country that has its own devils in the waters of boiling-over kettles. I lifted my hands to my face. Fat gauze clubs that smelled of roast meat, an odor that has sickened me since, as grease from a bit of venison was all Superior found to dress my wounds. That night in the convent bed, I knew God had no foothold or sway in this land, or no mercy for the just, or that perhaps, for all my suffering and faith, I was still insignificant. Which seemed impossible.

I knew there never was a martyr like me.

I was hollow unless pain filled me, empty but for pain, and yet the unceasing trial of my boiled hands was terrible. I cannot tell. There was no beauty in it at that level. I just endured. I was enfevered. The mystery of what I saw was some diversion. He crept in one night dressed in a peddler's ripped garments with a pack on his back full of forks, scissors, and paper packets of sharp needles. He tried them all out upon my flesh.

"Are you the Christ?" I screamed at last.

"I am the Light of the World," he laughed.

I thought of Lucifer. Even the devil quotes scripture to his own foul purpose. I was so frail on that bed, the sheets so overstarched their sound was magnified and their edges like blades, that I could summon no will to drive him out the window, or even crane my neck to see if he had a tail.

But then, hearing footsteps in the hall, he left on his own with no word from me, bounded out the way he came. I heard air rushing beneath his wide-stretched wings.

"We'll meet in the desert," he shouted before he vanished. I had to wonder. Which master had given me these words to decipher? I must hate one, the other adore.

Sister Saint Anne entered, bearing a full bowl of broth strained from the boiled fins, tails, and mashed bones of a carp.

"This will strengthen you."

She fetched a small three-legged stool, sat beside me, lifted the wood spoon to my lips. But the soup burned. I spat the first taste on the floor.

"Forgive me," said Sister Saint Anne. The spoon shook in her fingers and pink patches formed beneath her eyes, spread outward, leaving only the tip of her arched nose stark white. She was furious. I knew her well enough to read the evidence, but it must have been Satan trying his needles on me, poisoning my blood, because I could not stop my tongue.

"You stink," I told Sister Saint Anne. "You smell worse than this hell-soup does. Take the slop away."

Sister Saint Anne froze in the act of dipping from the bowl. Her face was tiny, sweet enough in prayer to break a wicked heart, but I was already pure.

"Open," said Sister Saint Anne.

I clenched my jaw, and won a form of triumph as she lost her patience, a venial sin that she must report later to Father Damien. She put the soup on the bedside table, rose and pinched my nostrils tightly. I struggled but could not fight her with my hands. I resolved, in those first seconds, to hold my breath. If I smothered, so much the better, as she would have the deep stain of my death on her soul forever, unconfessable perhaps, a mark that would seal her judgment.

I closed my eyes. In order not to breathe, I began to travel. But I would not take the three-day road, where I knew what lay ahead. I was forced to follow a path I didn't want—the turn-off that led into the woods. I walked, unwilling, the old way to Matchimanito Lake, passed the round slough and tall yellow reeds, over the tamped snow and grass through the massive oak trees, came to the clearing and continued away beyond Fleur's cabin until I broke from the undergrowth and stood on shore.

The lake was pounding, rolling, and the sky over me was dark, but light fell from the scales and gleamed off the tips of the horns when he rose from the water like a shield, like a breastplate, rings of iron in his skin and from his lips, clear fragments of jutting stone.

I must have given voice to some dreadful note. At any rate, I must have opened my mouth. For I was swallowing a sudden rush of salty fish broth when I woke, another and

194

another spoonful, until the bowl was empty and Sister Saint Anne gathered the satisfaction to beg my pardon.

"You were so ill you did not know what you were saying," she suggested.

I pretended a sudden sleep, but I did not rest. The desert was all around me and I knew which god was which. Christ had turned His face from me for other reasons than my insignificance. Christ had hidden out of frailty, overcome by the glitter of copper scales, appalled at the creature's unwinding length and luxury. New devils require new gods.

Dark from dark, I prayed, *True God from True.*

I asked for the place I might meet him, what desert and what land. Because my own God was lamblike and meek and I had strengthened, daily, on His tests and privations, it was I who was armored and armed even though my hands were loosely bound. It was I with the cunning of serpents, I with skill to win forgiveness. I was cleft down the middle by my sin of those days in Argus, scored like a lightning-struck tree. Deep inside, that crooked black vein, charcoal sweet, was ready to dissolve. If I did not forsake Jesus in His extremity, then He would have no other choice but to make me whole. I would be His champion, His savior too.

When I had puzzled out all of this, I slept without dreaming. I woke the next morning, drank the watery boiled oats Superior brought me, sipped the weak and unsugared tea from the cup she placed at my lips, prayed fervently after her and then received her blessing with humility. I tried to press my mouth to the hem of her sleeve, but my wrapped hands were too awkward to grasp the coarse material. Later, when the binding was excruciatingly changed, I shed a skin with the dirty wrapping. Every few days I shed another, yet another, and I drank or ate whatever my Sisters brought.

I fattened in bed, took on subtle heft. Fraction by fraction I increased in my Lord's eyes. New flesh grew upon my hands, smooth and pink as a baby's, only tighter, with no give to it, a stiff and shrunken fabric, so that my fingers webbed and doubled over like a hatchling's claws.

Then I went out. I didn't hunt like Fleur. I stayed in my own body and behind me in the spring mud I left only the tracks of my misworn shoes. Of course I prayed with every step of discomfort, but I addressed God not as a penitent, with humility, but rather as a dangerous lion that had burst into a ring of pale and fainting believers. I had told Superior this would be my one last visit to Matchimanito before the day of my entrance as novice, after which I would repudiate my former life. I knew I would not see Pillagers, Kashpaws, or old Nanapush again after that, and they would not miss me. I was pledged to a task, and when it was accomplished I would have no further use, or quarter, for this lost tribe of Israel.

They could starve and fornicate, expose their young for dogs and crows, worship the bones of animals or the brown liquor in a jar. I would have none of it. I would be chosen, His own, wiped clean of Fleur's cool even hand on my brow, purged of the slide of Napoleon's thighs, of Russell Kashpaw's hot and futile wonder, down in Argus, of the spikes of frost, the snow ferns that grew in Dutch James's hair, of Margaret's unbearable crane stews, of the infant's high wail after which I lay asunder. I would be free of Nanapush, the smooth-tongued artificer.

He had manufactured humiliations, traps. He was the servant of the lake, the arranger of secrets. Not one flare of belief lit his mind and he laughed too much, at everything, at me. For that I had no stomach, no forgiveness. So I did not even hesitate when I reached the south shore and a voice told me where the old man had hidden his patched boat. I pulled it from concealment and then searched the gravel edge until I found the right stone, one shaped long enough to tie properly and use in anchoring the craft. I fixed it to the bundle of rope he kept in the bow, placed it in the bottom and launched myself onto the lake.

It was a calm blue spring afternoon. I drifted halfway across, saw the Kashpaws scattered in the woods. Eli tossed Lulu up in his arms. Margaret sat by the shore and helped Nanapush draw fish from the margins of his net. When I was close enough to distinguish their voices, I lowered the rock.

Down it went. Down and down to where the thing was coiled, half-sluggish from the winter. In my mind, I saw the stone glance off its shoulder. One gold eye opened. I stood in the boat, my wool cloak gray against a change of sky. The blue brightened, drifted over with wisps of sparkling fog. The wind increased its spring blow. Slow-melting cakes and plates of ice bobbed in the waves. The lazy scoundrel's boat wasn't well caulked, for as soon as I'd launched, it had sprung leaks.

The water rose to my ankles. I prayed. The water stopped.

"Nanapush!" My call wavered, scattered by the breeze, yet they all stood motionless on shore now, looking and pointing. They were such small foolish sticks strung together with cloth that in the heat of my sudden hilarity I nearly tumbled over the side. I hadn't expected my main danger to come from the sight of their antics, but there it was, convulsions of mirth sent by the devil, spasms that started anew each time a figure on shore ran or wrenched its arms in circles. This was how God felt: beyond hindrance or reach.

And they tried. Over the hours, I witnessed their muddled attempts, the growth of a crowd of my sisters and our priest. Father Damien himself launched a small brown canoe into the waves, but God tossed him back on shore, sopping and endangered, for the water was frigid enough to still the blood. Theirs, not mine. I roared like a furnace when I laughed, and even the damp wool stayed warm against my flesh. I was important, beyond their reach, even Fleur's though she must have been hiding in the cabin, weakened by my act, for I caught no glimpse of her. I saw Napoleon stagger into camp with Clarence, and other riffraff followed. Sophie stood, ungainly, pale, dragging along the bastard girl she often cared for as Bernadette weakened. Marie.

I knew what Bernadette intended, I knew her reasoning. But I found my intention by remembering how I was forgiven of responsibility by Christ in the flesh. The child ripped herself from Sophie's grasp and stumbled toward the water's edge. She was thin as a rake, her black hair was wild as a tree in leaf, but they had left her that way just to tempt me, I knew, and I was not moved or swayed.

Kashpaws and Pillagers retreated and turned their backs on the growing crowd. Only Nanapush stayed, all rags and crooked poles, clever enough to maneuver the same canoe God had thrown back when it contained the priest. I prayed, as the rascal nimbly set out and righted himself wave after wave, that God lured him forward in order to overturn the vessel just out of land's reach. But he continued to make progress toward me, nearly capsizing several times, twice swirled entirely around so that his furious paddling, only, kept him upright and bound in the right direction. At last we were close enough to speak.

"That boat's no damn good, Pauline!" he yelled.

I scorned to answer, just balanced easily.

He drew closer, put the paddle in carefully beside him, held to the side of the spouting craft and bawled into my face.

"Come back with me, you stupid girl."

I lowered myself into a kneel, held my hands clasped. The bilge sank farther in the water.

"I shall not live by bread alone," I said.

"There's meat," he cried, swooping in the trough of a wave, "good stew!"

"I want words from God's mouth."

"You'll drown!"

"Get thee behind me," I muttered.

He heard. Hand over hand he pulled himself to the bow and steadied it. But I began to shift my weight, to rock, nearly tipping myself and him so that he must let go.

"Look on shore," he cried, showing me the kingdom of the damned, the living ones pointing in astonishment, staring with their chins dropped, their interest restirred by this drama. I laughed out loud, for there was Bernadette, holding to her face a small instrument that I supposed were her mother's tiny pearl opera glasses, brought all the way from Montreal in a trunk.

I tried to reach around and tug the paddle from Nanapush's hands so I could throw it aside as I had my own, and leave him to the mercy of his gods, but he retreated with an acrobat's grace, set out for shore. When he was gone I gazed into the feather clouds, watching for a sign, a promise, some answer which did not appear until I happened to see beyond him, onto the shore to where Fleur now stood, apart from them all, so gaunt and dark I thought at first she was a rain-dark young tree. Her back was turned.

I screamed at her, but the wind flattened out my words. Her figure swelled into relief, as if the force of my yell enlarged her. Her hair was covered by a scarf white and brilliant as the moon rising, and the ends of it whipped and fluttered at her neck. But the rest of her was planted tight. Her heavy black clothes, her shawl, the way she held herself so rigid, suggested a door into blackness.

I stood before it and then she turned, so slowly I heard the hinges creak. A moment and I was inside where I could not breathe and water filled me, cold and black water of the drowned, a currentless blanket. I thought I would be shut there, but she turned again and off she walked, a black slot into the air, a passage into herself. A crushing sadness. I was glad when at last night approached.

The waves tossed monotonously. There was no rain, though I gradually became soaked from the mist and spray. The wood of the hull swelled shut and sealed. I found a lard can attached to a string, used it, bailed. Across the water, their bonfires sprang against the trees. The shadows of their forms diminished in number as the darkness grew, and I was covered from their eyes. No one would dare to salvage me now. Invisible spars of jagged ice could tear a boat apart. I was safe, at least left to my purpose, which was to suffer in the desert forty days, forty nights, or as long as the patches lasted on this boat. I had determined to wait for my tempter, the one who enslaved the ignorant, who damned them with belief. My resolve was to transfix him with the cross.

The water numbed my feet, then the lack of feeling crept to my knees. I continued to pray but nothing happened. The waves swept around my boat, ice scraped against the hull or chunks knocked incessantly, then sank. The bonfires on the margin of woods died to aching glows. I wrung my skirt, chafed the blood back into my feet and legs, then lay down. I could pray just as well out of the cutting wind.

Then the thing below severed the rope of my anchor with its long saw-tooth tail, and began to tow me toward shore.

The boat traveled. The stars passed in a whirl. Wind caught my veil and chips from the crackling and singing ice glanced off my face. The waves slapped faster, but I stood, a figurehead. Held upright by the hands of God, I prepared myself to meet him without encumbrance. I stripped off my raiment, the veil, the shift and vest. I removed the stockings and the bandage that bound my breasts flat. The wind tore these costumes from my hands, cast them about me into the water as I approached the low and rippling fire, on fire myself, naked in my own flesh, and finally with no shield or weapon to confront him but the rosary I gripped.

I tumbled forward when the boat slammed on shore, scrambled upright on the balls of my feet, ready and strong as a young man. My unshorn hair lifted and fell about my shoulders, and all through me I felt the rocking of the lake.

"Show yourself!" I challenged.

And he did, having crawled from the water to confront me in that place. He reared, dropped a blanket set with mud. The fire glared into my eyes and the heat from his body flooded me. He was not huge, but large enough in the flicker of brass light, a man's size. I held the beads out at arm's length like a noose, and stepped forward. He retreated, filled his human-looking hands with small stones, and his mouth too, for I think when he spoke sheer black lake pebbles popped from his broad lips, striking me, burning with a hiss. There was an odd pleasure to the tiny stinging blows and in the words, which tightened me from nape to heels. I saw double, or not at all in the flickering glow. I felt his breath, a thin steam that swept along my collarbone and my throat as we crushed close. And then I seized him and forced myself upon him, grew around him like the earth around a root, held him still.

I strung the noose around his neck and counted each bead in my fingers as I tightened the links. He began to pound beneath me like a driving wind and I went dizzy with the effort of holding on, light and dry as a fistful of matches. He rose, shoved me against a scoured log, rubbed me up and down until I struck. I screamed once and then my tongue flapped loose, yelled profane curses. I stuffed the end of the blanket in his mouth, pushed him down into the sand and then fell upon him and devoured him, scattered myself in all directions, stupefied my own brain in the process so thoroughly that the only things left of intelligence were my doubled-over hands.

What I told them to do, then, they accomplished. My fingers closed like hasps of iron, locked on the strong rosary chain, wrenched and twisted the beads close about his neck until his face darkened and he lunged away. I hung on while he bucked and gagged and finally fell, his long tongue dragging down my thighs.

I kicked and kicked away the husk, drove it before me with the blows of my feet. A light began to open in the sky and the thing grew a human shape, one that I recognized in gradual stages. Eventually, it took on the physical form of Napoleon Morrissey.

As the dawn broadened, as the fire shrank and smoldered, I examined each feature and confirmed it for the truth. I felt a growing horror and trembled all through my limbs until it suddenly was revealed to me that I had committed no sin. There was no guilt in this matter, no fault. How could I have known what body the devil would assume? He had taunted me, lured me, shed blankets in a heap. He had appeared to me as the water thing, glass breastplate and burning iron rings. I could certainly prove that over doubt, for I was marked here and there, pocked as if we'd rolled through embers, stamped by his molten scales in odd reddened circles, in bruises of moons and stars.

There was hard work to do, then. I dragged him by the suspenders down a crooked path, into the woods, and left him in high weeds. They could find him or not for all I cared. I started to walk back toward the Mission, started running, and then I realized I was still naked, with no covering. I rolled in slough mud until my arms and breasts, every part of me was coated. I flung the beads high in a tangling arc toward the deepest brush. Then I stood. I was a poor and noble creature now, dressed in earth like Christ, in furs like Moses Pillager, draped in snow or simple air. God would love me better as a lily of the field, though no such flower as I had yet appeared on reservation ground. Again, again, on the way up the hill, I threw myself into the ditches. I rolled in dead leaves, in moss, in defecation of animals. I plastered myself with dry leaves and the feathers of a torn bird, saying that I would toil not nor spin for my supper, but live as sparrows, as mice, as the lowliest of things He loved, so that by the time I came to the convent, by the time I crawled and stumbled past the early risers, I was nothing human, nothing victorious, nothing like myself. I was no more than a piece of the woods.

I am now sanctified, recovered, and about to be married here at the church in our diocese and by our bishop. I will be the bride and Christ will take me as wife, without death. For I was caused by my sisters' most tender ministrations to regain my sense, to wash in the name of my Divine Husband, to eat His provender and drink His blood, so brutally spilled. In their kindness, they still tie on my shoes and watch until I've put each supper morsel into my mouth.

I learned a great deal from keeping my eyes closed these past months, and from listening to my sisters' idle talk. I know the Morrisseys found the body of the old drunk in the woods, behind Fleur's cabin, and that of course they blamed her for Napoleon's death. The Pukwan boy, now grown in influence, had long wanted to get even for his father's fatal illness, a Pillager curse.

I believe that the monster was tamed that night, sent to the bottom of the lake and chained there by my deed. For it is said that a surveyor's crew arrived at the turnoff to Matchimanito in a rattling truck, and set to measuring. Surely that was the work of Christ's hand. I see farther, anticipate more than I've heard. The land will be sold and divided. Fleur's cabin will tumble into the ground and be covered by leaves. The place will be haunted I suppose, but no one will have ears sharp enough to hear the Pillagers' low voices, or the vision clear to see their still shadows. The trembling old fools with their conjuring tricks will die off and the young, like Lulu and Nector, return from the government schools blinded and deafened.

I am assigned to teach arithmetic at St. Catherine's school in Argus. It is as if Superior knew, as if in this placement she sent me to atone. Yet she spoke in a kind voice, said that vocations such as mine are rare, and urged me to set an example for other girls from this region. I have vowed to use my influence to guide them, to purify their minds, to mold them in my own image although I do not like children very well, their scratching voices, eagerness, the way they bawl and screech. Through perseverance, I will overcome my instinct. I will add their souls to those I have numbered. For Christ's purpose is not for us to fathom. His love is a hook sunk deep into our flesh, a questionmark that pulls with every breath. Some can dull themselves to the barb's presence. I cannot. I answer with the ring of fidelity, with the veil. I will pray while my hair is chopped from my head with a pair of shears. I will pray as I put on the camphor-smelling robes, and thereafter I'll answer to the name I drew from Superior's hand.

I prayed before I spread the scrap of paper in air. I asked for the grace to accept, to leave Pauline behind, to remember that my name, any name, was no more than a crumbling skin.

Leopolda. I tried out the unfamiliar syllables. They fit. They cracked in my ears like a fist through ice.

CHAPTER NINE

Fall 1919–Spring 1924
Minomini-geezis
Wild Rice Sun

—

NANAPUSH

It began as a far-off murmur, a disturbance in the wind. We noticed an unusual number of birds and other animals that nested or burrowed in trees. Thrashers and grouse settled in the wild grass around Fleur's cabin. Kokoko silently appeared in broad daylight and walked the roof at dusk, uttering one note. Rabbits came to the edge of the clearing, squirrels bounded through the leaves, fighting pitched battles over territory. The murmur grew more distinct.

Then one day we could hear them clearly. Ringing over the water and to our shore came the shouts of men, faint thump of steel axes. Their saws were rasping whispers, the turn of wooden wheels on ungreased axles was shrill as a far-off flock of gulls.

Fleur dressed that morning, strapped on her skinning knife, and loaded her gun.

"Wait," I said. "Let me inquire first."

I walked to the settlement, and all the way there, in the homes where I stopped for water and talk, to try and discover the reason for lumbering, I encountered a silence. Those I thought of as friends turned their faces, too nervous to speak. Those I knew were enemies made no pretense at ignorance. They couldn't. Pukwan, Morrissey, the Lazarres I met along the road, these ones had no art to disguise the swelling satisfaction in their hearts.

And yet, I learned, the Agent was not against us. I entered his office and stood before his desk. I was told that it was not his fault the trees were sold and cut down. Nor was the tribe to blame. There was no adversary, no betrayer, no one to fight. Bernadette was friendly. The Agent smiled and spoke in a voice of pleasant softness.

"We had a very good bid on the land, a lumber company. The government is obliged to take an offer of that sort when the taxes are unpaid."

"Unpaid?" I shook my head. "But they were paid. I saw Nector Kashpaw with my own eyes; I saw his mother take the money in her hands. They walked to town with the priest beside them and left those coins and bills with you. The fee was settled."

"Oh yes," agreed the Agent, remembering. "The Kashpaws did bring a good sum to me, but you are mistaken about where it went. Nector and his mother paid that money down on the Kashpaw allotment."

He saw my strangeness, my astonishment, and continued smoothly. "We had to levy a late payment fine, of course, the money *was* tardy. I remember now, oh yes, they wrangled over it and Margaret, well you know her, such a shrewd woman. In the end it was settled and the money put down on the Kashpaw parcel."

I suppose I must have stumbled in my manner, for his answer sent me reeling.

The Agent pulled a chair away from the wall and motioned toward it. "Sit down, Grandpa," he said. He addressed me as an elder, yet he spoke as though I were a child. "Let me explain. The Turcot Company has, very kindly I must say, consented to start the lumbering operation on the far side of the lake. This will give the residents time to gather their possessions. Even time to build somewhere else."

His round face was slick and cool, his upper lip covered by a mustache of yellow hair. I watched the brush move up and down with each word, then I gripped my walking cane and spoke. I ignored the worst, for now, which was Nector and Margaret's decision. I concentrated on the man before my eyes.

"I am not your grandfather."

He laughed as though I had made a joke.

"How much was paid?"

"Oh a good deal, a good price, Mr. Nanapush."

I banged my stick next to his round-toed shoe. "How much of that good price, that illegal late fee perhaps, splashed into your pockets? How much is stored in the walls of my old cabin, which you gave Lazarres? How much cash did you stuff into the mattress of Bernadette?"

I swung my stick toward her, pointing it between her legs. But she stared at me without shame, and said, "Get out you old longhair."

On the way back to Matchimanito, my hip pained me a great deal and I rested each slow mile, examining the predicament. I now saw what Father Damien read, looking into a distance I could not have imagined. He was right in that I should have tried to grasp this new way of wielding influence, this method of leading others with a pen and piece of paper. I looked around. If I had, perhaps the road I walked would not have been rutted by the wheels of laden wagons. Huge wallows would not have opened where the crews pried loose from mud after a rain. The lumber men often used drags or sledges, and these too had cut the earth, as did the shod hooves of animals.

It was the death road of the trees and all that lived in their shadows. The sounds of men came from the east now, much nearer Fleur's cabin than they'd started that morning, it seemed to me. I gathered myself and walked with slow steps, turned down the old path. I knew I had planted the seed in Nector's mind when I told him that the wives of so many Indians now shared in their husbands' land. I know he paid the money down on Kashpaw land from foresight, shrewdness, greed, all that would make him a good politician. As he grew older, he resembled Eli more in face and less in spirit. Whereas the elder brother never lost his tie to the past, the younger already looked ahead.

My heart was on the ground then. I knew what was to happen.

Farther on as I neared Fleur's cabin, the woods were still untouched in sameness, so high, so cool. The wind in their branches was a shelter of air. I didn't know why I had ever found them frightful, why I ever wished to translate the language of their leaves. The path narrowed again and I felt my wandering relatives draw near, felt the rustle of their airy thoughts and complaints. I was lost in my arguments and wonder when a small wild girl with twigs caught in her hair ambushed me, held me by the leg and rifled my pockets for a drop of horehound. You were surprised to find nothing there, to hear no excuse. You grasped my hand and led me to your mother. Fleur stood on the shore, and even when I drew near to her she maintained a stillness, as though she knew what was to come. Her eyes rested on the far shore and she did not turn to me.

"Do you see anything?" I asked.

Fleur inhaled breath bitterly after a long silence, and muttered without shifting her gaze. "Nothing. What have you learned?"

Eli joined us, stood hunched in the shadow of a tree, waited for me to tell what, I understood then, he knew already.

And so, with the three of you standing there I told the story. I have seen each one of you since then, in your separate lives, never together, never the way it should be. If you wanted to make an old man's last days happy, Lulu, you would convince your mother and your father to visit me. I'd bring old times back, force them to reckon, make them look into one another's eyes again. I'd work a medicine. But you, heartless one, won't even call Fleur mother or take off your pointy shoes, walk through the tough bush, and visit her. Maybe once I tell you the reason she had to send you away, you will start acting like a daughter should. She saved you from worse, as you'll see. Perhaps when you finally understand, you'll borrow my boots and go out there, forgive her, though it's you that needs forgiveness, and you that will need a mother once the Morrissey fills you with child and whines in your ear and vanishes.

At any rate, on that day so long ago, I told Fleur everything as fast as I could with nothing held back. When my voice stopped I felt the awful relief of silence, then the fear of what Fleur would do.

From across the lake, there came a man's faint cry of warning, then a long snapping fall and the echoing boom as the length of a tree met ground.

Fleur bent over, picked some stones up, and dropped them into her pockets. She did not answer me. It seemed that she disregarded all I'd said, or perhaps did not believe it, her actions were so calm. She searched the smooth rocks piled around her, rejecting some and keeping others. I thought perhaps she was in a daze of pain, of helplessness. I tapped the ground with my stick to focus her attention. I thrust you into her line of vision. Eli found words of explanation. He seized on what Margaret had said long ago, about Fleur sharing the Kashpaw land if they were married. He crouched next to Fleur, crooned to her, touched her arms with his fingertips. I heard Nector's words about land value, and the convenience of a house nearer the crossroads, spout from his lips as well. Fleur's hands moved urgently, sorting stones from stones, and you helped her as though you knew what they were for.

"Father Damien will marry us without waiting for banns," he coaxed in a low voice. "My mother's house is small, but I'll add two rooms. Then I'll work in town, or I'll trap a hundred mink. I'll raise money, enough to buy a piece here. Only don't blame Nector. He's young, he's like my twin."

Fleur lugged a large flat boulder to her chest. She seemed to judge the weight of the rock, her eyes trained on the distance of water. She sighted along a line, a glint of sun toward the far side, where a drift of waves fell with peculiar force and regularity across a blue-gray horizon, crashing high into air. A spray of vapor lingered, caught trails of light, uncoiled.

I dropped my stick, leaned over and pressed my hand to Eli's mouth. With my other hand I tried to catch Fleur's dress, but she touched you as she passed and then walked into the water. The waves surged around her forceful steps, and the rocks in her skirt and the one she held to her breasts pulled her quickly underneath. The water closed over her head. She was nowhere, gone so suddenly that, out of disbelief, we stayed poised in the position we'd assumed. Eli came to himself first, ran to shore and pulled off his boots. He dove, thrashed to where she'd disappeared, and surfaced with one arm around her. Fleur dragged him down. From the disturbance of the water I could tell they struggled. Maybe Eli pried the stone from her arms and emptied her pockets. Maybe he punched her chin, knocked her out somehow, because she swallowed water and choked. Gripping her short, ragged hair, Eli dragged Fleur to land. I helped him roll her over on the bank, drowned and gray, and I ordered you to run to the house for blankets, anything so that you would not see.

There was an emptiness, an awful quiet to your mother, the sound inside a drum, and I said out loud, "This is the third time she has drowned." I forced myself to shake her face while Eli pulled on her arms. But when her eyes flew open, black as lake stones, sharp as ice, I leaned away from her at once. She rolled the water in her mouth one way, the other, spat it at us in a stream.

"Take your hands from me," she whispered. I grabbed at Eli, tried to drag him. The ground beneath us was trembling, I felt it shake, and it was not the felling of the trees or a storm gathering beyond sight, it was what was in the water, which I didn't dare to name. Eli, who had convinced himself that Fleur was no more than his wife, felt nothing but a husband's tenderness and fell upon her body with caresses and cries of love. She reared, grabbed his ears like the handles of a jug, and held his lips an inch away.

"*Nector* will take my place!" she hissed.

Eli tumbled backward when she let go, but Fleur didn't take her eyes off him. Her lips began to form a second curse and Eli rose to a crouch, gathered comprehension, stood, and did not turn but retreated from her presence. Each step he took became more definite. Though her face was alive, she was laid out like the dead, turned west, hands curled along her sides. She opened the Pillager smile, and Eli fled into the trees. From what I learned later, he ran straight to the lumber camp. Panicked to keep his word and repurchase the land, he hired onto a crew for a daily wage.

I remained after he had gone. When you came back with a blanket I wrapped you inside and told you to close your eyes. A moment later, you were asleep against my chest. The wind brought the sounds of wagons retreating, horses heading to their barns and pastures for the evening, men calling to each other in the rising dusk. We never moved. The wet clothing shrouded your mother's body like a sheet of weeds but she wasn't cold. I do not think she was in her body, not altogether, for it took a long time for her to answer when I asked if she would curse me next.

At last her lips opened, and she said she would not. She would curse the lumber bankers and officials in their nests and curse the Morrisseys. But never Nanapush. She propped on her elbows, hair in stiff spikes, and we regarded one another without moving until you talked in your sleep. I don't remember what you said, but I know it was ridiculous, and made no sense, and that it made your mother laugh.

She laughed out loud so rarely that I didn't recognize the sound of it at first, rich, knowing, an invitation full of sadness and pleasure I could not help but join. Then we were lost in it, rolling, waking you, unable to stop until Margaret's voice cut from the dark above us. She had come to take me home, or perhaps to find out if Fleur knew what she had done.

"What are you cackling about?"

We instantly ceased. Then Fleur spoke to me in a low voice.

"Go to her. She saved my life twice and now she's taken it twice back, so there are no more debts. But you, whom I consider my father, I still owe. I will not harm your wife. But I never will go to Kashpaw land."

I did though. Kashpaw land was good to me and took me in, although a change came about. I never believed the best of Margaret again, or loved her quite so much, perhaps, for in my heart I sometimes found that I envisioned a meeting with old Kashpaw, someday, in the land of the dead. First things first. We had to sort out the women we had loved between us. I saw us as old friends, clasping arms, smiling into one another's eyes. I heard myself make generous offers, and I heard him accept, even pictured Margaret in his arms. It caused me no pain. On the contrary, it sometimes made things bearable.

From her house, I visited Matchimanito often in those next weeks. That is how I came to be there when the surveyors found Napoleon. They had come into the densest woods, not far from the cabin. He was roots, stalks like threads, thin white blooms and blue moss. He was a powerful vine, a scatter of glowing mushrooms. But the Morrisseys recognized him by the red sash, unraveling strand by strand, carried half off by nesting birds. He was surrounded by acorn cups and bundles of twigs, all things we suspected you were afraid to explain that you had put there. No matter. The Morrisseys and Lazarres who naturally appeared had their story rehearsed even before they wrapped the bones and brought them to the Mission for burial in consecrated ground.

Not two days and that story was on every tongue. Once out, as if repetition equaled truth, it strengthened until the inventions were known as fact, until it came back reshaped and enlarged by a hundred pairs of lips: Fleur had killed Napoleon by drowning, just another in her line of men. She had discarded him, stolen his tongue. Wrapped in a fishskin and worn in her belt, it enabled her to walk now without leaving tracks. No one knew what else she did to him, or why, but the remains of her medicine were scattered everywhere—piled rocks, acorns, the screech owl's feathers. Worst of all, Napoleon himself soon came back and spoke to Clarence. He accused Fleur in a vision, one hundred proof and straight from the bottle.

More stories surfaced, swept mouth to mouth. Fleur had stationed her own dead child to guard Matchimanito. Napoleon had ventured beneath the shadow of its umbrella. And now, our tribe's policeman, Edgar Pukwan Junior, decided to conduct what he delighted in calling an investigation. It sounded so important, this long white word the war had taught him. He crept through the woods, watched our houses, appeared suddenly beside us and followed Margaret into church. Sometimes he sidled close to the confession box when she was inside, just hoping. I went in once and gave him something for his efforts.

"Father," I said in a loud voice that carried through the panels of chiseled wood, "I witnessed a terrible thing."

Outside, I heard the clumsy young man stumble close in eagerness, his breath hushed. I heard the others, too, stop their mumbled Hail Marys and cock their ears.

"I cannot hide it in my heart any longer."

"Yes . . ." said Father Damien, suspicious.

"It is about a young man, the keeper of law in our village. There is something strange with him ever since he has returned from France. They say he longs for a certain street in Paris, one that he has described to us. Whenever he gets lonesome for it he lies in the grass near people's cabins and Father, it is hard to say this, he makes love with himself."

There was silence from the other side of the metal grill, and from outside the tap of shamed, creeping feet, smothered laughter escaping from behind people's knuckles.

"I have an unusual penance for you," Father said at last. "Your sin is not the wrong of witnessing, but of divulgence. You will not speak a word for the rest of the afternoon."

Harsh punishment! Yet because of Margaret's watchful

amusement, I carried out my sentence and then exploded at dusk, when I began to speak and sing and couldn't stop even though my wife beat her head on the wall and then mocked me.

"Shaming a young man again!" she said. "What will you do when he takes revenge?"

"Out-talk him," I said, "or snare him like the other." But I remembered ourselves tied and helpless in the Morrissey barn. I sobered, thinking of the anger of Pukwan Junior. I had provoked it, fanned it to a blaze, but perhaps I was too mildewed and soft for it to feed upon.

Fleur was better fuel. Day by day, the rumble of the carts increased and now a barge was operated, pulled along one side of the lake by horses, filled with cut trees. These went to Eli, who worked as a log peeler and lived in a camp constructed on the far shore. Morrisseys and Lazarres worked there too, but never lasted long. Hired in the morning, they were ready to quit by noon, and notorious for sneaking off to sleep beneath the wagons. One was killed that way when two oxen lurched eagerly in their traces, and the wood fell from the unsecured hatch. A white man lost an eye when a splinter of wood spun off his axe. Two others perished, fallen from the lake barge or, some said, startled by the sight of Moses Pillager, who swam alongside, grabbed their ankles, pulled them under.

But no matter how many vanished, more came in their stead, and all of them had crosscut saws, sharp axes, and received for their pay both money and food. I thought that Fleur would fade now, react in dismay, that without Eli and surrounded by the lumber crews that labored with careless persistence, her heart would empty. I thought that since she had strolled into Matchimanito, determined to walk toward the cleft of bright water on the horizon, and since she had been dragged out by Eli, she would have no choice but to come live with us, to be there when Eli returned.

Instead, she took strength.

Perhaps she spoke too brightly, too easily, and showed insufficient fear now, perhaps she moved with too much youth and purpose for the situation. Thinking back on it I believe I did not watch her closely enough, observe the danger of her daily work around the cabin. I did not mark the way the pumpkins and squash she tended, in a raked plot of garden near the shore, flourished madly, almost in defiance, spread their leaves and blossoms. There were signs I never thought of as signs—the axe she'd obviously stolen, the edge of sawtooth metal jutting from beneath the house. Many times I had to wait for her when I visited, and when she emerged from the woods she was trailed by cats. Small mounds of sawdust drifted on the path I took. Woodchips littered the ground. Often, I smelled the spilled sap of pine. Fleur shrugged when I noticed these things aloud, mentioned some plan for building a cart, mumbled and hid a smile.

It was the other thing she did that gave alarm.

Because you think she gave you up willingly then, because she made you go, because you think she punished you for playing near a dead man in the woods, you turn your face and won't listen. Don't stop your ears! Lulu, it is time, now, before you marry your no-good Morrissey and toss your life away, for you to listen to the reason Fleur put you on the wagon with Nector, whom Margaret had hidden from your mother's wrath. She sent you to the government school, it is true, but you must understand there were reasons: there would be no place for you, no safety on this reservation, no hiding from government papers, or from Morrisseys who shaved heads or the Turcot Company, leveler of a whole forest. There was also no predicting what would happen to Fleur herself.

So you were sent away, another piece cut from my heart.

Perhaps you've heard what I'm going to tell now, I don't know. If so, you've heard it on the lips of others and never from one who witnessed.

After you were safe, Fleur came back to Matchimanito and stayed there alone, as she had when she was a girl. Margaret, in sorrow over Nector, picked quart after quart of his favorite juneberry and then filled our house with rich sweet steam of preserves and jellies. She'd give that boy anything, just like you. And he's still one too greedy for sweets, or so I hear. At any rate, there was a long period of unusual calm in the August weather, days in which no air stirred, no breeze foamed the lake. Even the clouds were changeless, the same ones visible at dawn as when the sun set. The sky hung daily overhead, a painted picture, motionless.

I was uneasy, lonely, and took the long way to visit Fleur. I was going there to talk about you. Since Pauline, my boat was useless, stove in so badly that weeds tumbled through the bottom, so I walked. Bad weather usually develops during daylight, but nothing about this weather seemed proper. Morning began with a greenish light. There was thunder in the distance, the smell of a storm drove me among the twisted stumps of trees and scrub, the small, new, thriving grasses which had been previously shaded. I passed through the ugliness, the scraped and raw places, the scattered bits of wood and dust and then the square mile of towering oaks, a circle around Fleur's cabin.

The moment I entered, I heard the hum of a thousand conversations. Not only the birds and small animals, but the spirits in the western stands had been forced together. The shadows of the trees were crowded with their forms. The twigs spun independently of wind, vibrating like small voices. I stopped, stood among these trees whose flesh was so much older than ours, and it was then that my relatives and friends took final leave, abandoned me to the living.

I saw my wives. Omiimii, the Dove, her little cries and her small unlucky face. Zezikaaikwe, the Unexpected. I touched the hands of White Beads, Wapepenasik, whom I'd loved painfully. I held our small daughter, Moskatiki-naugun, Red Cradle, whom I'd called Lulu. Our son Thomas, also named Asainekanipawit, Standing in a Stone, was there too. Old Man Pillager. Ogimaakwe. Josette. They were all gathered. Ombaashi, He Is Lifted By Wind, raised his hands running past, exalted, almost flying. I was with my father for a moment, Kanatowakechin, Mirage, as thick snow came down all around us, obscuring our trail, confusing the soldiers and covering the body of my mother and sister. I closed my eyes. I felt the snow of that winter and then the warmth of my first woman, Sanawashonekek, the Lying Down Grass. I smelled the crushed fragrance of her hair and full skirt. She took my arm, showed me how simple it was to follow, how comforting to take the step.

Which I would have done happily, had only the living called from that shade.

But Fleur had resisted these ghosts, at least she was not among them. So I would remain with the living too.

I passed wagons and men now, standing and shifting their weight or batting off the clouds of insects that descended in the windless, wet heat. They were waiting for the signal, for the word, to take down the last of the trees. I stepped as fast as I could go, and kept an eye out for Eli. I was sure he did not understand what was in store, not that I was any wiser, but the silence of the leaves and the long oppression of the weather frightened me. No bird clicked or whistled now. No animal rustled. No voices muttered in the shadows. No smoke came from the chimney of the cabin once I entered Fleur's yard.

Fleur was standing by the front door. I smelled the sharp, sour warmth of cats, and knew Moses had walked behind me and was hiding. The lumber crews were drawn up in a loose bunch at the edge of the clearing where Eli stood alone. The other men endured his sudden flow of words, chewed and spat impatiently. Their eyes were on Fleur. Eli had been appointed to talk her into leaving her cabin peacefully, and he was having a hard time of it.

Sweat glistened on his brow. His hair still hung long, held in a tail down his back, but he now wore a new shirt of checkered flannel and his pants were blue and stiff. Thick boots were on his feet. He held his hand out and said, "Come over here, we've got a wagon ready for you. I'll load it myself."

Fleur put her hands on her hips. Her black skirt and red blouse were worn so sheer that they clung like vapor to her breasts and waist, tied on with strips of floursacking. Her hair was thick, full of lights, falling in a wide arc. She wore no jewelry or feathers. Her legs were bare, her best moccasins, quilled in yellow swirls and flowers, were on her feet. Her face was warm with excitement and her look was chilling in its clear amusement. She said nothing, just glanced into the sky and let her eyes drop shut.

It was then I felt the wind building on the earth. I heard the waves begin to slap with light insistence against the shore. I knew the shifting of breeze, the turn of weather, was at hand. I heard the low murmur of the voices of the gamblers in the woods.

I turned to the men gathered, spread my hands in the air. "Go now," I said loudly. "All of you. Go!"

But not a one of them so much as flickered their eyes from Fleur.

And now, along the edge of the last high woods, a low breeze moaned out of the stumps. Fleur walked over and grabbed me, took my walking stick and dragged me to her tended yard. I looked around, curious as one becomes in moments of such tension. Perhaps I felt death near and wanted to impress a last vision behind my eyes. Slender vines of planted peas traveled along the foundation. Hills of rhubarb spread, quiet, a smudge fire smoked a hide, a small meat cache swayed on stilts, the polished stone where you liked to sit gleamed behind us. The stolen axe was planted in the dirt, the stolen saw beside it. I stared hard at these objects.

The men spun in surprise when the first tree crashed down beyond sight. Someone laughed nervously, another commented in rude tones and then there was a brief cessation among them. They listened. Fleur's hair ruffled and the hide across the fire flapped. Another tree, a large one, pitched loud and long, closer to where we stood. The earth jumped and the shudder plucked nerves in the bodies of the men who milled about, whining softly to each other like nervous cattle. They bit their lips, glanced over their shoulders at Fleur, who bared her teeth in a wide smile that frightened even those who did not understand the smiles of Pillagers.

One man walked quickly to the east, then stopped. A small tree went down and barred his path. Men climbed into their wagons, licked fingers to test the breeze. The next tree slipped to earth.

It was then I understood.

Around me, a forest was suspended, lightly held. The fingered lobes of leaves floated on nothing. The powerful throats, the columns of trunks and splayed twigs, all substance was illusion. Nothing was solid. Each green crown was held in the air by no more than splinters of bark.

Each tree was sawed through at the base.

One man laughed and leaned against a box elder. Down it fell, crushed a wagon. The wind shrieked and broke, tore into the brush, swept full force upon us. Fleur held to me and gripped my shirt. With one thunderstroke the trees surrounding Fleur's cabin cracked off and fell away from us in a circle, pinning beneath their branches the roaring men, the horses. The limbs snapped steel saws and rammed through wagon boxes. Twigs formed webs of wood, canopies laced over groans and struggles. Then the wind settled, curled back into the clouds, moved on, and we were left standing together in a landscape level to the lake and to the road.

The men and animals were quiet with shock. Fearing a

second blow, they lay mute in the huge embrace of the oaks. Eli sat on the ground, dazed, legs straight out, staring dumbly. Moses had paddled from shore. From behind the cabin, Fleur wheeled a small cart, a wagon that one person could pull, constructed of the green wood of Matchimanito oaks.

I looked inside the box of the cart expecting Fleur's possessions but saw only weed-wrapped stones from the lake-bottom, bundles of roots, a coil of rags, and the umbrella that had shaded her baby. The grave markers I had scratched, four crosshatched bears and a marten, were fastened on the side of the cart. We left quickly. The path was covered with debris. I helped her push over and around the trees, and together we made our way to the turnoff that had once been dark and now was filled with ordinary light, weak seedlings, flowered vines and leaves.

We stood uncomfortably together in the light. Fleur asked for my blessing, and what could I do but give it to her, like a father, although I did not want her to go.

When she buckled herself into the traces of the greenwood cart I said, "Stay with us." I got no answer. There was none that I expected. An extra set of moccasins and a thin charred pair of patent leather shoes were slung over one shoulder. Into her hair, grown thick again, she'd thrust the white fan from Eli, provided from my third wife's French trunk. Her earrings gleamed, the fan fluttered like a wing. The wheels groaned as she threw her weight against the yoke. She looked at me, her face alight, and then she set out. I stood in the middle of the path. I watched her until the road bent, traveling south to widen, flatten, and eventually in its course meet with government school, depots, stores, the plotted squares of farms.

After we knew Fleur was gone, and there was no telling when and if she would ever return, Margaret and I went after the authorities, put our minds to getting you back home. Nector chose to go south after he finished grade eight, even farther away than you, down to the state of Oklahoma. We did not give up. I wrote letters, learned to send them from Theobold or Hoopdance, as anything mailed through Bernadette never reached its destination. Margaret and Father Damien begged and threatened the government, but once the bureaucrats sink their barbed pens into the lives of Indians, the paper starts flying, a blizzard of legal forms, a waste of ink by the gallon, a correspondence to which there is no end or reason. That's when I began to see what we were becoming, and the years have borne me out: a tribe of file cabinets and triplicates, a tribe of single-space documents, directives, policy. A tribe of pressed trees. A tribe of chicken-scratch that can be scattered by a wind, diminished to ashes by one struck match.

For I did stand for tribal chairman, as you know, defeating Pukwan in that last year. To become a bureaucrat myself was the only way that I could wade through the letters, the reports, the only place where I could find a ledge to kneel on, to reach through the loophole and draw you home.

Against all the gossip, the pursed lips, the laughter, I produced papers from the church records to prove I was your father, the one who had the right to say where you went to school and that you should come home.

It was a dusty, blowing, and waterless day, when they brought you back to us. The year was 1924, and Margaret and I came to town in our wagon. We sat beneath a newly leafed-out cottonwood. Margaret's white hair was long enough to braid now. Her face had softened and folded, but her tongue had not dulled.

"This child better be the last you father in this tribe." The mocking way she dropped her gaze and smoothed her skirt across her knees made me want to reach for her. But too many eyes were pretending to look away from us, too many tongues were set like the wands of snares. And then the rattling green vehicle the government sent pulled in and jammed on the brakes in a cloud of grit. The air was harsh, sucking at the lakes and ditches in a threat of drought. Dazed children burst from the door.

You were the last to emerge. You stepped gravely down, round-faced and alert, so tall we hardly knew to pick you out from the others. Your grin was ready and your look was sharp. You tossed your head like a pony, gathering scent. Your braids were cut, your hair in a thick ragged bowl, and your dress was a shabby and smoldering orange, a shameful color like a half-doused flame, visible for miles, that any child who tried to run away from the boarding school was forced to wear. The dress was tight, too small, straining across your shoulders. Your knees were scabbed from the punishment of scrubbing long sidewalks, and knobbed from kneeling hours on broomsticks. But your grin was bold as your mother's, white with anger that vanished when you saw us waiting. You went up on your toes, and tried to walk, prim as you'd been taught. Halfway across, you could not contain yourself and sprang forward. Lulu. We gave against your rush like creaking oaks, held on, braced ourselves together in the fierce dry wind.

Louise Erdrich

The Bingo Palace

Seeking direction and enlightenment, charismatic young drifter
Lipsha Morrissey answers his grandmother's summons to return
to his birthplace. As he tries to settle into a challenging new job on
the reservation, he falls passionately in love for the first time. But
the object of Lipsha's newfound obsessive desire, the beautiful and
enigmatic Shawnee Ray, is in the midst of deciding whether to
marry his boss, the wealthy reservation entrepreneur, Lyman
Lamartine. Matters are further complicated when Lipsha dis-
covers that Lyman is his rival in more ways than one. In league
with an influential group of aggressive businessmen, Lyman has
chosen to open a gambling complex on reservation land – a
development which threatens to destroy the community's funda-
mental links with the past . . .

'Erdrich is so thoroughly in tune with the surreal poetry of America
that when you read her you can hear America singing, the choruses
of its multitude of voices, its rough music.'   ANGELA CARTER

flamingo

Louise Erdrich

The Beet Queen

'A perfect and perfectly wonderful novel.'   ANNE TYLER

On a cold spring morning in 1932, two children, Karl and Mary
Adare, leap from a boxcar. Orphaned in a most peculiar way, Karl
and Mary have come to Argus to seek refuge with their aunt
Fritzie. So begins this exhilarating tale, spanning some forty years,
and brimming with unforgettable characters: ordinary Mary, who
causes a miracle; seductive, restless Karl; Sita, their lovely,
ambitious, disturbed cousin; Wallace Pfef, a town leader who
bears a lonely secret; Celestine James, Mary's life-long friend; and
Celestine's fearless, wild daughter Dot – the Beet Queen.

'Violent, passionate, surprising . . . small towns, the prairies,
sexual obsession – all the matter of the classic American novel.
The Beet Queen imparts its freshness of vision like an electric
shock.'   ANGELA CARTER

🏭 *f l a m i n g o*

Louise Erdrich

Love Medicine
New and Expanded Edition

'The beauty of *Love Medicine* saves us from being completely devastated by its power.'
                                                          TONI MORRISON

Set on and around a North Dakota reservation, *Love Medicine* tells of the intertwined fates of two families, the Lamartines and the Kashpaws. The women at the heart of this extraordinary community are survivors in a harsh and tumultuous world, united and sustained by the strength and diversity of their love – the sweet delusion of the flesh; the powerful pull of blood ties; the affection for the old ways vying with the irresistible lure of the new. Their voices mingle and blend to form a continuous braided sequence of narratives which pulse with the sheer energy and drama of life.

'The impression is of a river of memory busting its banks and overflowing upon the page in an irresistible flood.' ANGELA CARTER

🏰 *f l a m i n g o*

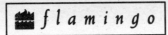

flamingo

Flamingo is a quality imprint publishing both fiction and non-fiction. Below are some recent titles.

Fiction
☐ No Other Life *Brian Moore* £5.99
☐ Working Men *Michael Dorris* £5.99
☐ A Thousand Acres *Jane Smiley* £5.99
☐ The North China Lover *Marguerite Duras* £5.99
☐ Dancing in Limbo *Edward Toman* £5.99
☐ Split Skirt *Agnes Rossi* £5.99
☐ The Great Longing *Marcel Möring* £5.99
☐ The Sandbeetle *Zina Rohan* £5.99
☐ Miss Smilla's Feeling for Snow *Peter Høeg* £5.99
☐ Postcards *E. Annie Proulx* £5.99

Non-fiction
☐ Language of the Genes *Steve Jones* £6.99
☐ Dr Johnson & Mr Savage *Richard Holmes* £6.99
☐ Other People *Frances Partridge* £7.99
☐ Cat Among the Pigeons *Alice Thomas Ellis* £5.99
☐ In Ethiopia with a Mule *Dervla Murphy* £6.99
☐ On the Side of the Angels *Elizabeth Smart* £5.99
☐ The Runaway Brain *Christopher Willis* £6.99
☐ Wild Swans *Jung Chang* £7.99

You can buy Flamingo paperbacks at your local bookshop or newsagent. Or you can order them from HarperCollins Mail Order, Dept. 8, HarperCollins *Publishers*, Westerhill Road, Bishopbriggs, Glasgow G64 2QT. Please enclose a cheque or postal order, to the order of the cover price plus add £1.00 for the first and 25p for additional books ordered within the UK.

NAME (Block letters)_____

ADDRESS _____

_____